NEW ΓO THE NEIGHBORHOOD

KATHERINE KIM

This is a work of fiction. Names, characters, places, and incidents either are the products of the author's imagination or are used fictitiously. Any resemblance to actual persons, living or dead, businesses, companies, or events is entirely coincidental.

Follow me on Instagram @katherineukim or on Facebook www. facebook.com/katherineukim

Cover by Enchanted Ink Studio

Editing by Robin J Samuels www.shadowcatediting.com

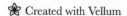 Created with Vellum

For Curtis and Jared. You're both way funnier than I am.

Keep up with new releases, giveaways, and other antics by joining my email community. You'll get news of releases, a free short story, updates from any shenanigans I get up to, and all sorts of things! Otherwise you might consider looking at my Patreon page, where you will get advance access to short stories and sneak peeks at my novels!

MOVING PAINS

"**M**om, I'm not moving back to Nebraska, please stop asking me to." Theo sighed silently and squeezed his eyes shut. There was a headache starting to form right behind his eyeballs. He scratched his fingers through his hair and then down through his short beard as she kept talking.

"I just hate that you're so far away," his mother said as if he weren't fully aware of that already. "Your father and I miss you at Sunday dinner."

"I miss you guys, too, Mom." Theo had to smile, despite the impending migraine. "But you know why I can't stay there."

"I suppose," she said with a sigh. "But there must be better places to be than Whitelake. A real city with better access to the scientific community."

"Yes, Mom. They tend to be more expensive places, as well. And I don't need to live near the people I interview. I can email or call or video chat with them or see them in person at a conference. Just like I have been doing."

Theo slumped over to lean an elbow on the kitchen

counter and stared out the window over the sink. The backyard was a bit weedy after what Theo assumed was months of neglect. A service came in and mowed last summer, then cleaned everything up in the autumn. That was it, though, since most of the intervening months had been winter, and there was no need for a lawn service.

His mother kept up her argument as Theo's eyes traced the edges of what must have been a nice little garden border, now full of dead leaves and some scraggly bushes that he couldn't identify, backing up to a chest-high wooden fence. The house sat high enough that it was easy to see over the fence from where he stood, which seemed a bit like cheating, but Theo loved it.

Past the back fence was a narrow path popular with joggers, dog walkers, and other assorted morning people, and past that, the silver glitter of the river. Watching the sunlight shimmer off the slow moving water soothed him somewhat, and the contrast with the dark shadows under the trees of the forested parkland on the other side calmed something in his psyche. He took the benefits it offered without looking too deeply into why he felt so strongly connected to the place.

"Theo? Doesn't that sound better?"

Theo had no idea what his mother's suggestion had been. Not that it mattered.

"I like it here, Mom. It's quiet. I can write. And now that I finally have the bank sorted out, I can really just focus on my book's outline," Theo said. "You've wanted me to get this book published for a while now. Well, now I can get back to my routines, stay quietly by myself, and work on it without distractions. No surprises."

Distractions like his ex-friend Jerry trying to call him every day to make excuses and talk him out of selling his half of the business. Or like Penny's friends being extremely passive-aggressive when they saw him at his favorite coffee shop, snubbing him for dumping her–people he had thought of as his friends, as well, but apparently not.

It was fine. He could live here and get his book together and be much more productive. Develop his own routines without having to worry about accommodating anyone else. He already had a few routines, in fact, despite taking the morning off to deal with the bank.

"I suppose I can understand that. If it's going to be like a writing retreat so you can focus I suppose that makes some sense." His mother sighed. "But Theo, you be careful. That old man was unhinged. He most likely ought to have been in care somewhere with people who could have a psychiatric eye on him. Lord knows what's in that house or who he encouraged to come around."

"Mom, Great-uncle Garfield has been dead for almost a year. I'm pretty sure his friends know by now." Theo dug a thumb into the corner of his eye. The headache was growing.

He had already spent almost an hour on the phone with the bank that morning, fixing the screw-up that was preventing him from updating his address. Thank *god* he hadn't combined his finances with Penny. Ugh.

"Look, Mom," Theo cut off whatever else she had been about to say. "I need to go. I'm getting a headache and if I don't take something right now it's going to flatten me and I won't get any work done. I love you guys and tell Dad I'll write him an answer to his email soon. I want to really be able to focus on it, and today's not looking good on that front."

"Okay, honey. Make sure you eat something healthy. Remember, good food feeds a strong mind!"

Theo couldn't stop the small smile that the familiar phrase evoked.

"Yes, Mom. Bye." Theo thumbed the end call button and slumped fully onto the counter.

He had only been there for two weeks and this patch of the counter, the table behind him, and the bed in the guest room were the only surfaces that were fully cleared off. Thus this was currently his office. Every other horizontal plane in his great-uncle's house was cluttered with knick-knacks and books and things that as a little boy–the one time his family had visited–he had considered the most amazing treasures. Shells and feathers and acorns and interesting pebbles and coins from all over and bits of broken jewelry.

He couldn't tell his mother that he still sort of thought they were treasures. Just... really disorganized treasure. A bit like a magpie's nest. Although, real magpies were no more likely to make off with bits and bobs than any other critter on earth. Still, to paraphrase Dickens: the wisdom of our collective ancestors was in the metaphor, and Theo's unhallowed hands shall not disturb it. He was going to have to clean out the house eventually. It was not a task he was looking forward to, but there was an unfamiliar spark of excitement in his belly when he thought of what he might discover.

His head throbbed, bringing Theo back into the moment. He had best get some painkillers and a large glass of water and try to get to work. He had taken the morning off to deal with the bank and that was done now, and the call to his mother to cool off hadn't worked out quite as well as he hoped it would. She was usually good for a calm, rational discussion, but today had been more about reopening wounds that had barely had time to scar over.

He swallowed the pills and was about to walk through his kitchen door to stand on his back deck, take in some sunshine regardless of the chill, and hopefully recover from the morning when the doorbell rang.

There was no way that whoever it was needed to see him. It was probably some salesman or someone else who hadn't heard yet that Great-uncle Garfield was dead. Just as he finished that thought, there was another ring, followed by a chipper but insistent knock.

With a sigh, Theo went to answer the door.

On the other side was a blonde woman in a very expensive variation on the soccer-mom look: pristine designer jeans, a pale-pink button-up shirt under a puffy down-filled vest. Gold jewelry with a huge, flashy diamond settled next to a diamond-studded wedding band that she was careful to wave in such a way to catch the sunlight and sparkle. All of which he could identify thanks to Penny. Theo blinked at his visitor's carefully lipsticked smile and wondered who the hell this woman was, nor why she was glaring at a cat that perched on the railing by the stairs.

"If you're looking for Garfield McCann, I'm afraid you're too late. He's dead," Theo said by way of greeting.

"I am aware, yes. His loss was such a tragedy for the neighborhood. You are the new owner of this house, then? Did you buy it as is?" she asked as if she had any right to know. She peered around him, trying to see inside, and Theo shifted to further fill the doorway.

"I am."

She waited a moment to give him a chance to answer her second question, but Theo just stood there and out-waited her. Her plastic smile shrank slightly.

"Well," she said, and refreshed her smile. "My name is Marielle Trevor, and I am the president of the Green-woods Homeowners Association." She held out her hand, clearly expecting some form of deference. Theo took her hand, gave it a perfunctory shake, and let go.

"Theobold Warren."

He had vaguely known that there was an HOA here, and had been since some developer bought up all the empty land and a few older houses. They built a bunch of the boring boxes marketers called "attractive single-family homes" that Theo thought were bland as hell. He hadn't given the HOA any thought after the estate lawyer finished telling him about it.

The existence of the new houses, however, was also what gave the new residents the ability to form an HOA that included all the older homes, since they were all mixed together, and included a park and some other amenities that Theo didn't care enough about to remember, since the older houses were grandfathered *out* of a number of the regulations. And frankly he didn't care enough about trash cans to argue. He set an alarm in his phone and called it good enough.

"It's good to meet you, Theobold. I hope we can be friends." She smiled widely and leaned toward him just a bit.

Yeah, he didn't think so. Even if he were inclined to add people into his new life right now, they wouldn't be entitled, manipulative women. He'd had enough of that with Penny, thank you *very* much, and he hadn't moved over a thousand miles just to hang out with another one.

"I just wanted to stop by now that you've had a few days to settle in. I was expecting a moving truck or some such, but I suppose if you bought the house with all the furnishings included, you would need to clear it out first. Mr. McCann was quite the collector, I understand." She peered over his shoulder as if she would get an invitation to come in and explore a house she had clearly been denied access to. Theo wasn't about to break that streak. "Bit of a hoarder, even, I'd bet."

"Indeed."

"You're more the strong, quiet type, aren't you?" She smiled at him attempting to sweeten his disposition with a little flirting. Theo was not even considering being interested. "Not one for being chatty."

"Not unless I'm being paid by the word, no."

"Oh, are you a writer then?" She perked up a bit and leaned in. "Have you written anything I would know? I am a secret romantic thriller novel fan. Don't tell anyone, I'd be so embarrassed!" She tittered and waved her bejeweled hand in front of her face as if to ward off any potential teasing. "Well, I just wanted to come by and welcome you to the neighborhood and make sure you had my phone number. And I don't know if Mr. McCann left a copy of the HOA rules somewhere you can find them, or if the real estate agent had a copy to give you, so I brought you one. We take neighborhood cohesion very seriously. We like to make sure our community is attractive and pleasant, you know. My phone number is in there. It's my cell, you can call any time you want."

Theo simply took the thick packet she dug out of her bag. The thing was ridiculous. And heavy.

"I see."

"Really, I mean it. Anytime. I want to be available to anyone who needs me since I'm responsible for the whole neighborhood. It's such a serious honor, you know, and I take it seriously. Which reminds me, I know Mr. McCann had a service come out and do the yard work, but I wonder if the contract lapsed when you took up residence. Such a tragedy, to die alone like that, poor man. Anyway, I noticed that the grass is getting a bit wild out here, so you should make sure to get after it before you need a machete! I

tucked the contact information for the HOA-recom-
mended lawn service companies in the back there." She
tittered again and Theo wondered if that sound could be
considered torture under the Geneva Conventions.

He glanced at his lawn. It looked perfectly fine to him
for early spring. Just starting to really grow now that the
days were warming up. Sure, it could use a mow, but otherwise, it just looked like a lawn.

"I'll see what the estate lawyer knows," he said. He
wasn't about to promise this woman anything. Everything
about her gave him the creeps.

"Oh, and you might want to watch out. There seems to
be a vandal in the area. I saw *graffiti* on the forest bridge
yesterday! I called the police to report it immediately, of
course, and then I called the city since that is technically
city property, and they said they would send someone out
to paint over it soon, but you know how these city people
can be. So slow." She scrunched up her nose in a way she
probably thought was cute, but just made her look like she
was sniffing a garbage can. "There was some over by the
shops the other day too. A *tag* I think they're called. And a
friend of mine was mugged the other day! *Mugged!* Here in
Whitelake! Though not actually in our lovely neighborhood at least. You can rest assured that the Greenwoods
neighborhood is a safe one, even if there are a few, hmmm,
unusual residents. I even spoke to the most professional
detective the other day! I didn't even know that policemen
were so charming. Not at all rude and unkempt like the
ones on TV. Such a relief!"

Theo just stared at her. No doubt any cop this woman
liked was nobody Theo wanted to deal with. Fortunately
he was unlikely to ever have to.

"Well, I won't take up more of your time. Have you not
started your new job yet? I know moving can be so diffi-

cult, but I heard that you were from out of state, so I guessed that you hadn't started work yet, since you've been here during the day since you moved in." She tipped her head and smiled again.

"I mostly work from home. Speaking of which, I need to get back to it."

"Oh! That's right, you said you were a writer. How exciting! I do hope you'll let me know when your next book is out!" She tittered again and stepped back to wave before turning and strutting down the path to the shiny black SUV parked directly in front of his house. As she pulled away he noted the stick-figure family on the back window, including two tiny dogs.

Theo watched her drive off before grunting. Good riddance.

"Well, that was about the most entertaining thing I've seen all week."

Theo turned to look for the speaker and found himself staring back at the laughing face of his new neighbor, sitting on her porch. Theo sighed. It looked like he wasn't getting to his writing today after all.

2

BEING NEIGHBORLY

"So you met Marielle at last, huh? Lucky you." His neighbor was an older woman of some sort of Latin heritage, though Theo had learned never to assume anything. She was dressed impeccably, in black slacks and a bright blue twinset, her dark hair pulled up into a bun. She swept an assessing gaze over him and he felt like he was being judged. Not for wealth or status like Marielle had done, but for the quality of his soul. A shiver ran up his spine.

This woman managed to give off an air of friendly competence, however, not one of entitlement, and when she nodded slightly he blew out a breath in unexpected relief. His neighbor, at least, seemed to be made from real stuff, and irritating her would make his own life harder than necessary. He stepped off his porch and over to the side of his own yard, so neither of them had to shout. He rested his hand on the short fence—he had a white picket fence, now!–and greeted his neighbor.

"Good morning. I have met her now, yes."

"You're the nephew, then?"

He nodded. "Yes, ma'am, great-nephew. You can call me Theo."

She smiled at him and it was the sort that lit up her whole face. "Oh, such nice manners! But none of them for Marielle, I noticed."

He had nothing to say to that. He hadn't been especially polite to the woman and didn't regret it.

His neighbor's eyes twinkled, and laugh lines formed. "You seem to be a good judge of character. That woman is trying to run everyone out if they don't satisfy her personal vision. She'd have me out in a heartbeat if she could. I've got more money and better lawyers than she does, though." She laughed. "My name is Ivette Olivar. My family has been here for generations now, not that she cares. All she can see is my mother's Mexican genetics. That woman could no more run me off than she could order the sun around. She tries anyway. I'm not surprised she was all smiles for you, though. Handsome young man moves to the neighborhood? She may be married, but I can't blame the woman for appreciating nice scenery. And she likely thinks you'll fall into line easily enough."

Ivette winked at him and Theo felt his face heat.

"Um, thank you." Theo blinked. "Can she actually *do* anything? If we don't abide by the rules?" He hefted the packet of paper he still held.

"She can levy fines against you, and you'll note if you read that manifesto she handed you that those fines will accrue interest for every day they go unpaid," Ivette said. "She can threaten legal action, but my lawyer says that she can't do anything much beyond making a nuisance of herself. Though the sort of harassment she can dole out can be fairly awful. That woman." Ivette shook her head slowly. It seemed to be a significant condemnation.

"Houses like ours, the original ones, we get all sorts of allowances and exceptions. Marielle hates that."

"Basically she can try to annoy me out of my home?" Theo asked.

His new neighbor laughed and he couldn't stop a smile from starting on his own face. It felt foreign, like a half-forgotten skill. Maybe he didn't mind making one new friend, after all.

"That's about the size of it," she said. "Mind you, that woman knows how to harass. If this weren't such a good place for our people many would have gone long ago just to be rid of her."

That was an odd thing to say, but Theo supposed he could understand the sentiment at the end of it.

"Well, ma'am. You're not the only one with lawyers. I think I can manage Marielle," he said. Then he glanced around his yard and shrugged. "It's not really a big deal to get the lawn mowed though. She's probably right about it being a mess, I'm not a good judge of that sort of thing"

Ivette laughed again. "You read that novels-worth of HOA rules she's come up with. Then you'll understand that even something simple as mowing your lawn can be a trial. Even the biblical Job would have started grumbling if he had to deal with that woman."

"Fantastic," Theo sighed. "She did mention some drama going on, though. A mugging?"

"Yes, the vandalism and poor Colleen got assaulted by a nasty-sounding fellow," she said. Her expression lost its merry tone and her gaze got sharp. "I admit, I don't much care to have people coming into the neighborhood and poking around, especially a detective that Marielle feels cozy with. I haven't seen any of the vandalism myself, but I have a bad feeling about it all."

"I'm going to have to agree," Theo said with a sigh. He

pursed his lips and eyed the novel's worth of HOA rules. "As much as I don't like the idea of criminals running wild around here..." He let his words trail off, unwilling to speak so firmly against a woman he had barely met. He wasn't so blind to his own biases as to ignore the probability that he was taking out some of his irritation with his own recent past on the irritating Marielle.

Ivette tipped her head to the side and studied him, her brown eyes sparkling again and a small smile on her lips. She brought a hand up to run her fingers over the tasteful pearl necklace at her throat and after a moment she spoke again.

"I like you, young Theo. You came as a child to visit and I liked you then too, much more than your cousins. You've grown, but I think maybe you still have some growing left to do."

"Excuse me?" Goosebumps tingled over his arms at her words. And he was thirty-one years old, thank you.

"I may not have my grandmother's gifts, the blood is too thin now and I take after my papa's family too strongly, but I have learned over my long life to trust what my gut tells me. You are going to be good for this place–I know it. But I think this place is also going to be good for you."

Theo blinked at her. "Um." The goosebumps seemed to grow goosebumps. "Well. I guess I had better get back to work," Theo said.

Ivette nodded, a twinkle in her eye. "You don't write thriller novels, do you?"

"No, ma'am," Theo said. It shouldn't feel so much like failure to say that. "I freelance, mostly. Science articles for the layman and so on, a little ghostwriting. I am writing a book, but it's about the changes in archaeology over the past twenty years in reaction to the massive changes in the political landscape. It will be written for the dabblers and amateur history buffs rather than scholars and policy wonks. But it's in very early stages yet."

"I look forward to reading it."

Theo pasted a smile on his face. He had to start actually working on the damned thing first. "Well. It was nice to meet you."

"And you as well, Theo. I'm very glad that it was you Garfield chose. I think he made the right decision." And with that second odd statement, Ivette turned to pick up the book she had sitting on a small table by her elbow.

Theo went back inside and let the HOA rules book land with a thud on the table beside his laptop. The jostle woke the screen and he found himself staring at the outline for his book. It was something he had started working on just as a way to put his thoughts in order, but then Penny had seen it one day and mentioned it to his mother, who latched onto it like it was his crowning work.

Naturally, the next time Mom was in the same room with his agent at a small conference for science educators in New York, Mom had told Abby all about the wonderful book Theo was working on. Which, of course, had resulted in a long planning call with Abby, who drew up a timeline for publication and got working on all the contracts. And now he had a book to write.

Theo was exhausted just thinking about it.

But there was no avoiding it. The throbbing in his head had dulled to more of an ache, so he refilled his water bottle and took a deep breath, and sat down in his chair. He rolled his shoulders and positioned his fingers over the keys and found his eyes drifting over to the window. He could just see the top of his fence from here, and the sparkling sunlight on the river.

Theo took a deep breath and let it out slowly. Then he did it again and tried to focus on the scent of the coffee, the cool air on his face, the chirp of birds in a nearby tree. A robin landed on his back lawn and hopped around, looking for whatever it is that robins look for. Worms, he guessed, and turned to finally pour himself a cup

How his life ended up here, he still wasn't completely sure. Thirty-one years old and starting completely over fifteen hundred miles from the city he had spent most of his life in, living in the house left to him by a relative he barely knew, and writing a book he had never planned to write.

The bitter taste of the coffee when he poured it seemed to sink into his bones. He wasn't bitter himself—well, okay, he was extremely bitter that the woman he had spent almost a decade with turned out to be such a selfish jerk, and that his closest friend was a lying bastard. But the rest of it? His mother and her expectations were not so outrageous, really—a solid career grounded in facts and science, even if he was writing about it rather than doing the actual research himself. It wasn't an unreasonable thing for a parent to push for.

I need to get over myself, he thought with a frustrated growl. He was an adult now and just wanted to avoid people for a while. He was very clearly not the greatest judge of character, after all. Theo turned to glare out the window again.

Across the river, movement in the shadows of the trees caught his attention. Two young men stomped along the opposite path. The one in the lead seemed older for some reason Theo couldn't put his finger on. He was scowling and his tattooed arms seemed to flash and writhe in the speckled sunlight filtering through the trees and reflecting off the water. He was saying something to the man following him who struck Theo as somehow innocent, which was more than a little ridiculous considering his company.

The man in the lead was nearly bald, only a faint smudge of darker skin over his scalp and down his chin gave any clue as to whether it was natural or shaved. He wore a baggy sleeveless shirt, despite the chill still in the air to show off the tattoos and the nascent muscles, and equally baggy jeans. Theo couldn't help but describe him as having an air of darkness around him.

The younger man, on the other hand, was slim, possibly even underfed, and his artfully ripped skinny jeans only served to highlight that. In contrast to his friend, the blond's hair was wild and a bit shaggy, and he wore a hoodie over his T-shirt, the material almost swallowing him up rather than showing himself off. He was practically jogging to keep up with the older man's strides as he listened.

Theo frowned. There was something about the contrasts between the two that made Theo pause. Goose-bumps tugged at his skin as the pair vanished beneath the trees and he wondered what the younger man could possibly want with the bald one. It seemed dangerous, somehow, and Theo found himself tempted to head out, across the footbridge, and seek the two men out.

And do what? They were total strangers and there was no reason for him to get involved, and the impulse itself was bizarre. He chalked it up to the constant interruptions of the morning. It wasn't any of his business.

Theo dragged his gaze back to this screen which had gone to sleep while he daydreamed. *Focus, Theo.* He had taken the morning off to deal with the bank, and that was a good thing, but now he had to settle down. He'd had his lunch and now he needed to put all his interruptions behind him.

Outside, a crow called, and somewhere farther off a dog barked. Distant honking reminded him that there was a large road not too far away. The image of the young man, trying to get his companion's attention, and the deliberately continued ranting of the other drifted into Theo's mind again.

The laptop's screen went dark again and Theo slumped in his chair. If he kept letting himself get distracted, he would never get any work done.

3

BREAK TIME

Theo gave up. After all the interruptions and stress of the morning, his concentration was shot. He kept catching himself daydreaming and staring out the window at the sparkling water and the mid-afternoon sunshine. At least his headache had faded.

He got up to pace around a bit, maybe just a few minutes of daydreaming in the peace and quiet would settle his brain. The house was a dusty mess, though. While there had been a service that came to mow the lawn last year, nobody had been inside since Great-uncle Garfield had died. Not for any longer than it took to get him buried, at least.

Theo wondered for a moment who that had been. The lawyers hadn't gotten in touch with him until after the funeral, as per the instructions in the will, which made Theo sad. He hoped that the man hadn't been alone. That thought naturally led back to his mother's phone call and her rant about the house and about Great-uncle Garfield had him pacing aimlessly around the rooms downstairs, poking at dusty knickknacks and blowing great billows of dust off books. He picked up a small box and it clunked when something inside slid around, a sound that jogged a memory loose.

"Do you want to see something cool?" Great-uncle asked. His eyes were bright and sparkling, which Theo had learned meant something fun and exciting was about to happen.

"Yeah!" Theo agreed easily. Coming here, to this weird house full of treasures was the best idea his parents had ever had. He was still shocked that his mother allowed them to stay there instead of getting a hotel or something, but she had grumbled something about grant money and pay freezes. Whatever. He didn't care. Great-uncle Garfield was awesome.

"Here." Great-uncle held something out for Theo to take.

It turned out to be a box, made of wood with some sort of metal inlay patterned across it, and when Theo turned it over, it thunked.

"It's a puzzle box," Great-uncle said. "But not just any puzzle box, one that only opens when you know the right magic."

Theo turned the box again and that enticing thunk sounded. Whatever was inside was reasonably heavy and slid around freely. He chewed his lip for a long moment, running his fingers over the inlay and considering the edges and corners.

"Mom says magic is made up. That it's one of the top two preferred lies told by weak-minded people. Right up there with religion." Theo didn't think his religious classmates were particularly weak-minded. Or the kids who liked to read those books about the kids who have gods for parents, either.

Theo wasn't allowed to read those books. They looked kinda cool, though.

"Your mom..." Great-uncle's voice sounded sad. "She has opinions, and there's nothing wrong with that. Many people see magic and dismiss it. Some trick of the light or they imagined it, or it didn't actually happen, they will say. But you and me, my boy..."

Great-uncle whispered some words that seemed to slide off Theo's memory and the box popped open, clean down the middle like one of those nesting dolls. No latch or trick or anything, even the metal inlay looked like it had always been seamed there when Theo knew it had been one solid piece a moment ago, and inside was a cream-colored stone. Theo tipped the box and caught the stone in his hand, the rounded edges and off-center point making it look like a wobbly heart drawn by a child.

"What do you think of that, my boy?" Great-uncle asked, almost glowing with excitement. "You can keep that stone. For luck!"

Theo blinked at the similar box in his hand and turned it over, making whatever was inside this time clunk solidly. Frowning, he popped the lid open. Another rock sat inside—this time a piece of quartz, clear as glass. Theo frowned and put it down on the table in what would be the living room once he cleaned it out. He grumbled as he left the room, a small part of his brain wondering where the puzzle box had gone.

A walk in the fresh air would do him some good. It was too easy to become sedentary as a writer. Besides, if the day was still as beautiful as it had been that morning, then he was in for a treat. The real question, he asked himself as he pulled on his jacket, was did he head for the hiking trails in the woods behind the neighborhood, or did he wander around the streets?

He remembered hiking with his mom when they had visited here all those years ago. Great-uncle Garfield tried to entertain his young guest with magic tricks and fantastic fairy tales of magic in the modern world, talking about it as if he had been there and seen the magic happen in front of him. One too many tales of *"I* remember the time when my friend*"* did something fantastical, and his mother had quickly decided that he needed to be kept away from the house and the imaginative old man, and firmly grounded in *reality*.

He hadn't thought it was too odd at the time—he had

only been eight, maybe? But looking back and knowing his mother, he realized that Garfield's love of fantasy made his deeply science-based mother very uncomfortable. Still, the woods were a wonderful place for a kid to explore even if his mother had kept up an ongoing commentary about life cycles and habitats and food chains, and Theo had fond memories of them.

He stepped outside and locked his door behind him, firm in his decision to put off sorting and remembering and all of it. Instead he set out to learn more about the town he had relocated to. It had changed since he was a child, after all. Not only thanks to the developer that came in, but the street just outside the mostly suburban neighborhood had seen new businesses move in and older businesses freshen up to match. There had to be some gems out there.

At least somewhere to get a decent cup of coffee. He glanced at his watch. *Or a drink and some food. And another drink,* he groused to himself. He walked out his back door and out the back fence, and down the walking trail for a short bit, just to get his blood pumping. The small trail was a cheerfully casual path, worn down by many feet tromping along heedless of the possibility of falling in, and he had the sudden image of kids playing along the bank of the river in warmer weather, chasing each other with laughter in the wind, only to turn and leap into the water and splash those still on shore. In his imagined scene, dogs leaped and barked and then jumped in too, following their kids anywhere and everywhere.

At the footbridge over the river, he turned left, back into the neighborhood. As he wandered back towards the main street, he took a real look at the houses he passed. It was easy to pick out the newer ones. They had no real soul to them. The older houses all had mature plantings and lush gardens in the front.   Hedges, and rope swings hanging from tall trees.   Porches with potted plants or decorative details. A few had sitting areas like his and Ivette's houses did. One had a very attractive pond with a cascading waterfall.

The new houses were... *sterile* was the only word that Theo could think of. Flat, untouched lawns kept trimmed very short.   Hyper-landscaped strips that they probably called gardens that all had the same two small bushes and a set-out pattern of bedding plants, that all had at least two feet of mulch between them, all in the same three colors. No trees in the front yards here.

He frowned at the flat green expanse of lawn next to him, thinking of his image of the river for a moment. Broad, shallow, and slow-moving behind the Greenwoods neighborhood, it was almost an ideal summer adventure for kids.   Theo glanced at the nearest house, one of the blank-faced boxes the developer had installed and then grumbled to himself, "assuming the children here are allowed to play at all."

Whatever, it wasn't any of his business. He turned and made his way to the road that would lead him out of this neighborhood of contrasts.   It was a warm day for February—he could almost have been out without his coat, just a good sweater and a scarf in the winter sunshine—but nobody was out in their yards. *Probably all at work*, he thought. *Or at school.* The only people likely still home were the people like Marielle who had taken on the job of minding everyone else's business.

Theo stepped at last onto the sidewalk outside the suburban wilderness and turned toward the area he vaguely remembered as having restaurants. At the time he had passed them he had been most concerned with knowing where the gas station and the grocery were, and had idly noted them to check out later. Well, now it was later.

He *didn't* remember the traffic being quite so heavy that day, though. Nor so loud. Or angry. Horns blared as people tried to navigate the thick knot of vehicles. The whole mess made Theo more glad than ever that he lived in walking distance.

Theo couldn't see any reason for the traffic snarl. The stoplight nearby seemed to be in perfectly good working order, and nobody was blocking the intersection. Maybe there was a problem near the bridge over the river. He couldn't see it, as the street curved away and there were too many houses between him and the water now, but that was more than likely the issue.

He crossed the street and made his way past a bar that looked like it had been there for decades, one of those community cornerstones that adapted to tolerate the nearby college kids. The sign caught Theo's attention and he considered the Three-Legged Wolf. The slightly old-fashioned sign swung in the slight breeze, showing a gray wolf, missing a front leg, staring calmly out as if to challenge him to discount the creature for its missing limb.

Perfect. Theo grinned to himself. Even better, at this time of day in the middle of the week, he wouldn't be surrounded by partiers and drunks like he would on the weekend. Perfect for a late lunch. Some flesh and blood people to offset his memories and the chance to fill his stomach with something comforting and not *too* healthy.

Perfect.

4

THE THREE-LEGGED WOLF

Theo stepped inside, and when his eyes adjusted he took a glance around, absorbing the unusually cozy atmosphere. Cream walls and dark wood were the two main backdrops for the decor, which was a mix of old photos and posters for local bands that presumably played on the small stage on the right wall. Tables ringed an area that was meant to be a dance floor, and booths lined the walls. Against the far wall on the other side of the dance floor was a long bar, behind which, among all the bottles and glassware he expected, was a large, framed grainy photo of a wolf with only three visible legs, standing over what looked like a deer and peering at the photographer.

It was still early for the dinner or after-work drink crowds and there were only a few people scattered around at the booths and tables. One pair of women was sitting at the bar with plates in front of them. Theo headed that way, assuming that was the best place to get served, despite the lack of a bartender. Just as he took a seat on a stool several spaces away from the ladies, the door to the right of the bar swung open and a man stepped out.

"Hey there!" the man said cheerfully, putting a crate down on a small counter behind him and turning to stride over.

Theo had to blink. For all that the man was tall, and broad with muscle, there was something... something odd about him. Theo blinked, his mind supplying an image of the bartender standing in the deep woods with dawn sunlight spearing through the leaves to light him up in the morning mist.

Theo shook his head to clear the bizarre image from his mind. It was probably brought on by the bartender's aqua-colored hair. Theo hadn't ever understood the phrase "an unruly mop of curls" until this very moment, and the magic forest prince image was only emphasized when the bartender broke out in a puckish grin.

"Hey there," he said again, stopping in front of Theo and propping a foot up on something behind the bar. "Long day? You look a bit spaced out."

"Um, yeah. Not long, just mind-numbingly dull, punctuated by irritating and unignorable interruptions." Theo finally pulled himself back to the present. "But fortunately it's over now, I hope. Is there a menu or something?"

"Sure. First time here?" the guy asked. He turned and grabbed a plastic-covered menu from a stack to the side and put it down on the bar then turned to grab a glass of water to put on a napkin. "Passing through or working at the college?"

"Neither, actually. I just moved into my great-uncle's house a few weeks ago." Theo waved vaguely in the direction of home. "I don't go out much, but after this morning I needed something…well…something not entirely healthy, you know? And noise."

The bartender nodded. "Gotcha. Then, welcome to Whitelake. Comfort food is so named for a very good reason. And if you mean Garfield McCann's place, then I'm actually one of your neighbors. I live a few blocks over with my cousin Darren, who you will no doubt meet soon. He was over there all the time with Garfield, pawing through the library and dissecting old events." He reached over and offered his hand. "Avery Steele, nice to meet you. I'm sorry for your loss. Garfield was a good man."

"Theo Warren." Theo's hand tingled where their palms had touched and he felt goosebumps prickle over his skin. He had been feeling that a lot since he moved, but not quite this sharp. "I didn't really know him well, to be honest. The call from the estate lawyer was a real surprise."

"Hey!" one of the ladies called out. She glared at them. "Flirt on your own time. We'd like some drinks now."

"Right with you." Avery turned back and sighed. "They're on the HOA board."

"Ah. I had the pleasure of meeting Marielle Trevor just this morning." Theo shuddered and tried not to roll his eyes. "Better go deal with them before they call the police to complain about the service or something."

Theo rolled his eyes. "Spoken like someone who's had the experience."

Theo shrugged in acknowledgment, and Avery smirked and headed off to take the women's order.

Theo scanned the menu and made his choices quickly, which left him plenty of time to stare off into space, and watch Avery move around behind the bar. He moved with a spare grace and economy of movement that made Theo want to say "like a dancer" but something about that thought didn't ring true.

Avery returned with a wink to lean against the back shelf with a bottle of water of his own, and Theo glanced over to see the ladies with fresh glasses of wine and sour expressions.

"So, you have experience behind a bar?" Avery grinned.

"Worked my way through college as a barista." Theo smiled slightly at the memory before a few in particular popped up.

His phone chirped and he glanced down at the text. He groaned and opened it up to read it when he read the preview text.

MOM: *Hi sweetie. Just ran into Penny, and she asked after you. Can't imagine why she would bother, as closed-minded as she turned out to be. Still, I did say that I would pass along the message, for what it is worth. She seems to be seeing someone new. I'm sure you could move back soon if she's moved on.*

Theo sighed and scrubbed his hand over his face.

"Whoa. That looks like bad news." Avery raised his brows and Theo caught the glint of metal from a piercing he hadn't noticed at first. "I come back here to swap crazy bar stories and get your order and instead you look like you just lost your job."

"I just want the cheeseburger and a beer, thanks, whatever's good on tap. And considering I'm a writer working on a book, losing my job would be tricky." Theo tried to smile but was pretty sure it came out as a grimace. "However, getting a text from my mom that manages to combine a guilt trip for moving away and a reminder of why I left is easy as pie."

"Oof, that's harsh." Avery turned to the computer at the side of the serving area and tapped a few buttons before grabbing a pint glass. "My folks hardly ever get in touch since I pissed off my dad by refusing to sign my life away to the Marines like he wanted me to. Still, when I do hear from them it's a long afternoon to recover, so I feel your pain." He put the now-full glass down on the bar and Theo contemplated it.

"She's just..." He frowned at the beer, took a sip and he held that thought. "Damn, that's good."

"It's a local brew. Basically only sells here at the Wolf, but if you're lucky you can buy right from the brewer himself. The owner's his buddy."

"Nice. I'll definitely have to remember this one." He took another long drink and put the glass down on the napkin. He had no real explanation for what he said next. "Mom means well, and she misses me I guess. She just managed to stir up a ton of shit with one little text." Theo was not inclined to talk about himself, but the words seemed to tumble out without his permission.

Avery cocked an eyebrow, the small ring through one of them twinkling.

"If you want to talk, I may just be filling in for the regular bartender, but my ears work just fine."

Theo shrugged. Maybe it was the bartender-confessional angle, but he *did* feel like he could tell Avery despite just meeting him. The goosebumps and the... the sense of otherworldliness about the guy settled something in Theo. He knew he could trust Avery with his sob story.

Well, at least some of it. It wasn't something he enjoyed talking about, though, which is why his mother didn't know the whole story—didn't know that the "someone new" Penny was seeing was his ex-best friend.

Also, there was the whole *safety* aspect of the conversation. The reason that Penny gave him to excuse her behavior. The cliché, outdated stereotype bullshit she had spouted still rang in his ears. "*Well you're probably out there sleeping around anyway, so what does it matter?*"

Stupid as hell that was even still a concern in this day and age, but humans were amazing at treating each other badly. Just another reason not to follow his mom's suggestion of making lots of friends. He was better off on his own.

Still, the words seemed to pour out of his mouth without consulting his brain. "My mom ran into my cheating ex and needed to tell me about it." It was the truth if only a small part of it. Fortunately, Avery had given him an excellent option for diversion. "You're just filling in at the bar?"

Avery grinned and Theo suspected he knew avoidance when he heard it, but he answered the question. "Yeah. The guy who's usually here in the afternoon had to call out today 'cause his kid's sick. I'm usually on the door in the evenings for security, but I worked my way through school at any job I could get, so I have enough experience to pitch in on occasion without making too much of a mess. The mid-week afternoon crowd isn't too challenging."

"And you said you live with your cousin." Why did Theo remember all of these details about a virtual stranger?

"Yep. Darren's just enough older than I am that he was renting a house already when I needed a place. He was finishing his PhD at the time and I basically paid rent by making sure he ate and had clean clothes." Avery laughed at the memory and winked when Theo laughed.

A faint buzzer went off and Avery held up a finger before heading off. He came back with Theo's meal then made the rounds of the bar, checking in with the other customers, including the demanding women. How that man could be a bouncer was beyond Theo's imagination. Sure, the guy had a somewhat athletic build, but he was still slim and spritely. "Lithe" was the word Theo would use if he had to sum Avery up. Nowhere near as big as one expected from someone in security.

Besides hair the color of the Caribbean ocean and the eyebrow piercing, Avery didn't particularly stand out in a bar like this. He stood just about the same height as Theo's own five foot eleven. The man's shoulders were broad enough and, sure, muscles were peeking out from the black T-shirt with the bar's logo on it, but they weren't obvious like you expect from a bouncer. And that grin was entirely disarming. There was nothing about the guy that was even a little intimidating.

Theo understood the man not wanting to join the military. They had just met and already he knew that the military was no place for Avery. The fanciful thought about elves and forest princes flashed through his mind again for a moment before he shook the thoughts free and focused back on his meal.

Theo ate in peace for a while, enjoying the food, which was exactly what he had wanted after that morning. Hot and cheesy with just the right amount of greasiness, and the fries were crispy and perfect. There was a scoop of coleslaw, too, that was zingy and still crisp and rounded the meal out just right. He was almost finished with his food when Avery came back.

"Hungry then?" He took Theo's glass and refilled it with a wink and a cocky grin. "On the house. Welcome to the neighborhood and sorry today was tough."

"Cheers!" Theo accepted the glass and saluted Avery before taking a sip.

5

DANGEROUS NEIGHBORHOOD

Theo spent the rest of the afternoon at the Wolf, as Avery referred to it, chatting with the man until it got too busy and the regular evening bartender came in. Theo finished his beer and wandered around the internet on his phone while he absorbed the atmosphere of the place, cozy and comfortable and filled with regulars heading in for dinner by the time he left.

He shivered in the cooling air. Winter was reclaiming the area after being driven off for a while by the spring sunshine, but he was still comfortable enough to feel like taking the long route home. Considering how many people he had dealt with over the day, and how irritating most of them had been, Theo was surprised at how relaxed and content he felt. Unlike the angry honking and snarled traffic in the road in front of him. Apparently, the commute around here was worse than he thought.

The Three-Legged Wolf was definitely someplace he wanted to go back to. Maybe he could take his laptop and work on a long afternoon when he felt like he needed to be social-ish. Hopefully, the regular bartender was as pleasant as Avery. Theo honestly didn't see himself coming back when Avery was scheduled to man the front door, though. Weekend party crowds weren't his thing.

Theo rolled his shoulders and meandered down the street toward the corner, buzzed enough to pay little attention to the traffic, which was still strangely snarled. Tired-looking commuters sat in their cars and glared at the stoplight and each other. The shop fronts he passed were warm oases of light, windows full of purses or shoes or whatever else they sold.

One shop—Forgotten Treasures—had a display of all sorts of antiques, plates, and furniture. To one side of the window was a charming tableau of a vintage purse, a pair of glasses, and a clock on a small wooden side table, looking for all the world like some young flapper was just home from dancing the night away. Tucked beside that was a sign with the shop's hours and a note that appraisals were available by appointment or walk-in. Theo made a mental note to go back and talk to them when he started cleaning out the house.

The flash of yellow spray paint against the darker bricks of the alley he approached caught his eye and he frowned at it. The shape was several concentric swirls with a spike stabbing through it, the paint sprayed with a heavy enough hand that it dripped and made Theo think of blood. He shivered and his stomach turned at the... the *wrongness* of the design.

Theo huffed out a hard breath, frustrated with his wild imagination today. Shaking his head to try to dislodge the strange whatever-it-was that was setting off the odd thoughts, he stepped forward. Before he had even taken two steps, he was yanked into the alley and shoved chest-first into the rough bricks.

"Gimme your wallet," a voice growled in his ear.

Something sharp pressed into his shoulder. "Make any noise and I'll put you down, Picket Fence."

"Sure, man. It's in my pocket. I'm just going to reach for it." Theo's heart was about to punch right through his chest, it was pounding so hard, but he kept his voice as steady as he could.

As Theo moved, slowly, he tried to remember everything he had ever heard in passing about surviving a mugging. There wasn't a lot, but he figured panicking and freaking out wasn't going to help. The mugger had shown a surprising amount of intelligence by shoving him into the section of wall hidden behind the corner of a small dumpster. Theo could see over the top, but only just, and in the dusk light and the jagged shadows in the alley, nobody passing by would ever see them.

"Hurry up. Hanging out with soccer dads isn't my idea of a good time," the mugger growled.

Theo moved slowly, trying to telegraph what he was doing. "I'm not any kind of dad, soccer or otherwise, but I get it. I don't have a lot of cash on me, though, and I just ordered new cards to make sure my ex has no access to the accounts, so fair warning."

The thug made a disgusted sound. "Whatever. I know all about people like you. Saw you making nice with that rich bitch this morning." The thug spat, barely missing Theo's shoe. "Now hand it over and maybe I'll leave your face pretty."

"Hey!" the voice rang down the alley like a gunshot, and the weight pressing Theo into the wall was abruptly removed.

Theo turned to see Avery standing between him and a lanky man wearing a ski mask and a hood pulled tight over top of it. Something about the mugger felt familiar but it was probably just the central-casting feeling of the whole scene.

Avery, on the other hand, damn near shone in the fading light, his body held loose but ready, and he radiated leashed energy. Theo couldn't see Avery's face, but something about it must have been a clear warning because the thug snarled and took off the other way, toward the access road and parking behind the row of stores.

Avery didn't move except to watch the mugger's retreat, and as soon as the man disappeared around the corner he relaxed, turning to Theo.

"You okay?"

"Yeah." Theo blinked. He was entirely sober now, the pleasant buzz from just a few moments ago long gone. "I didn't realize that there was a lot of that here. I spent all my life in a city, and never got mugged, but I move to the suburbs and within a month..." He brushed at himself, mostly to assure himself that he was still whole and unharmed.

"Hey, you're shaking," Avery said. "You're not hurt or anything?"

"No. Maybe some bruises, but I don't think..." Theo mentally checked himself over. "No. I'm okay. I've never heard someone use 'picket fence' as a derogatory term before, so hey. I learned something." Theo shook his hands out to try to stop the trembling. How Avery had seen it he had no idea.

"Okay. Adrenaline and shock, then. That's a better alternative than an actual injury. This is usually a pretty safe area, do you want to call the cops?"

Avery reached over and rubbed a comforting hand over Theo's shoulder, and he was damn glad for the contact.

"Probably should, huh?" he sighed. "Dammit. Today's been almost entirely unpleasant."

"I hope that I didn't make the list of the unpleasant things, at least. Come on, let's go wait in the back of the Wolf. It's quiet and you can sit down, then I'll walk you home, okay? Safety in numbers and all that." Avery gently guided him to the side entrance of the bar and unlocked it with a key to let them through into the hallway. The noise of the main room was muted here, the clanging of pots and the hiss of a fryer much louder. They passed a cluttered office and a very tidy storeroom before turning into a small lounge across the hallway from the kitchen.

"I'll go grab you some water and call the police. Do you want to see a doctor or something?" Avery asked once Theo was settled on the ancient sofa.

"No," Theo answered. "No, I'm okay, just rattled. Thanks."

Avery nodded and stepped across to the kitchen door and disappeared inside. Two hours later, Theo had given his statement and had a cup of coffee strong enough to stand a spoon up in, clearly from the pot they kept for the staff. Avery stuck around, not hovering, but checking in frequently to make sure that Theo was comfortable. The uniformed cops that took his statement frowned as he related what happened, but they wrote everything down and one of them went to investigate the alley as well.

Avery related how he had just left the bar and turned down the street to head home, only to see Theo get yanked into the alley, and explained that he had more than enough training to confront a single street thug. He gave the name of a martial arts school near the college where he taught, and the name of his contact at the community center where he gave self-defense lessons for free, so that the police could verify his claims.

Once they left, Theo asked him why they needed to know all that personal information, and Avery smirked at him.

"Did you see their faces when they heard I scared the guy off? Guys like that don't look at me and see someone who can handle a fight. They look at me and see a young punk kid who's more likely to get killed *making* trouble than successfully helping anyone." Avery shrugged but his eyes sparkled. "Looks can be very deceiving."

Theo just shook his head and huffed a laugh. "Apparently."

"Come on, let's get home. I called Darren to let him know I was running late, but he's probably forgotten completely. He had that 'I'm deep in my research' voice which means it's hit or miss that he was even aware that he was on the phone."

Theo laughed out loud that time. "He's that bad?"

"Very absent-minded professor when he gets in the flow." Avery nodded with a chuckle. "Not a lot of scholars in my family. Just him and my uncle that I know of. The rest of us were all warriors, so I'm not even sure if that's typical or just Darren." He held the door open to let Theo back out into the night. "I doubt the guy stuck around. There's two cop cars here now, and I know I've seen some detective guy talking to Marielle and a few others, so there's folks out, watching."

Theo tried not to let the dark unnerve him, but it was a close thing. Avery patted his shoulder and turned to pull the door shut. He hoped Avery didn't notice the way he flinched slightly at the quiet snap of the latch engaging behind them.

"Darren and I are about two blocks past your place. I'll walk with you."

"Thanks." Theo ducked his head and turned away from the door. Avery waited for Theo to start walking before he followed just a half step behind like he was Theo's bodyguard.

"So that's why your dad wanted you in the Marines, huh? Was he one, too?" Theo hoped he wasn't being nosy, but honestly, he needed the conversation to distract him as they walked down the same stretch of sidewalk. The angry traffic seemed to be finally clearing and the street was much quieter.

"Yeah. Dad was..." Avery grimaced and Theo was suddenly sorry he'd brought it up again. "Dad's stubborn, and while Mom sorta understands where I was coming from, she stands by him. My siblings are pretty cool though, and they help where they can, so it's not like I lost my whole family out of it. My oldest brother is actually the one who encouraged me to just *be* me, which I didn't expect back then. I just don't really talk to them much and, you know, it can be lonely sometimes."

"Well, you have Darren, right? And maybe your uncle, too, it sounds like?" They passed the alley with not even a hesitation. The graffiti had been scrubbed at as well, some sort of solvent smell hanging heavy in the air. Quick work, that.

"Yeah," Avery sighed. "Still miss Mom's hot chocolate and cookies. Best thing ever to come home to in winter. I can't get the cookies right, even though she sent me the recipe. She's a bit less rigid than Dad is since it was her brother that was a scholar, not a warrior, and my 'little rebellion' wasn't nearly as shattering to her side of the family." Avery sighed. "And Dad was pretty cool when I was a kid. It wasn't until I hit high school that he started in on the relentless military career path planning. My older siblings were already falling in line with it, you see. Marines, Navy. The whole shebang."

Theo blinked. They got across the street and the cat that had been hanging around his house off and on was sitting on the short wall that ran along the sidewalk here, separating the neighborhood from the rest of the street. It stood and stretched and hopped down lightly to rub against Theo's leg and saunter along with them.

"You get along with your siblings?" Theo asked. The shaky feeling in his chest was fading, and he rather suspected that Avery's presence and chatter were why. He would have to go back past that alley in the daylight as well, to banish more of these shivers, but for now, the company and the conversation were working their magic.

"Oh yeah. Two older brothers and a sister. She's a Navy SEAL. Totally badass. I can't even blame Dad for being insanely proud of her. Do you have any idea how rare that is?" The pride in Avery's voice was unmistakable. "My brothers are no slouches, either, though Alec got injured and had to come home. No amount of combat training can help when you're blown up. He works for the family security firm though, so he's okay. Mostly does training and logistics, because of his leg. They'll all work there when they're done serving."

"Oh wow," Theo said. "So your dad wouldn't even let you work for him? Had to be the Marines or nothing, huh?" He snuck a glance over at the man.

"Or the Army, or the Navy. Didn't much matter as long as it was active military. He was very insistent." Avery had his hands stuffed in the pockets of his leather jacket, his lean form hunched a bit as he spoke. "Says the only place I could 'learn to stand as a warrior' was the military, despite the fact that I've been training literally since I could walk and hold a sword at the same time."

Avery's tone had turned bitter. "I told him that I didn't want to be involved in the political mess that is the U.S. military, that I wanted to protect people with my skills, and he dug his heels in and, well...Now I'm here in Oregon, and they're mostly still in Virginia. My siblings are pretty cool, though. A bit snarky, but I'm the baby of the family, so they've always been kind of jerks to me. I know they have my back. I see them once in a while when they've got leave or something but can't get across the country from their base. Video chats."

"Wow. And I thought my mom was putting pressure on me. She just doesn't like me living in Great-uncle Garfield's house," Theo stumbled over the words, rushing them together. "That is a mouthful. Great. Uncle. Garfield."

Avery laughed, and the tension left his shoulders. "Sounded to me like you said *Gruncle* Garfield."

Theo chuckled. "And a new title was coined. From now on he shall be known as my Gruncle."

They were still chuckling as Theo stopped at the bottom of his porch steps. The cat jumped up to sit primly on the porch railing and started washing its face.

"Hey, thanks for your help," Theo said. "Not just with the mugger, but with getting my mind off everything."

"No problem, I'm just glad I could be there," Avery said with a shrug. He grinned. "It's what I do, you know?"

Theo chuckled. "Well, you're good at it. Don't let anyone tell you otherwise. Your dad doesn't know what he's talking about."

Avery stood a little straighter and his puckish grin faded to something a bit softer. "Thanks. You okay now?"

"Yeah. Goodnight." Theo waved as Avery headed

back down the path to the sidewalk and then off down the street.

The cat meowed softly then leaped into the wicker chair, settled down on the cushion, and started purring. It looked for all the world like a miniature Sphinx guarding Theo's front door.

"Yeah. Me too, kitty," he said and unlocked the door. "You have a good night."

6

THE NEIGHBOR KIDS

Theo could let the fear of being mugged keep him inside the house, or he could gather his courage and go for a nice walk in the sunshine. He stepped out his back door and startled the cat, who had been lounging in a patch of February sun on his deck. It shot him a disgruntled glare and stalked off the deck and around the corner of the house.

"Sorry to startle you! Thanks for keeping watch!" Theo called after the disappearing tail before striding across the lawn to the small gate that led out to the informal trail along the river. Joggers were a common sight there on the few mornings he woke early enough, and after yesterday's excitement a bit of soothing fresh air to start his day sounded like a good idea. Even if it was a Saturday.

Not that he was going to do anything insane like take up running before dawn, but a nice walk to start the day off wasn't too taxing and would keep him from seizing up in his chair as he worked. The woods across the river were full of life, he had discovered, and not just of the human variety. So far, when he stared out the back window while waiting on the coffee to brew, he had seen foxes and deer and had heard the distinctive tatta-tatta of a woodpecker echoing on one soft gray morning when he was up earlier than usual.

Today he was up at a *reasonable* hour, though, and most of the joggers and other morning denizens of the path were at work, or well into their day, and the foxes and deer were back in the shadows of the woods, safe from prying human eyes. He stood a good chance at having a pleasant walk. The solitude, and the opportunity to gather his thoughts and get himself ready to sit down and work, were both more than welcome. There was a lawnmower humming somewhere in the neighborhood, and the faint sound of traffic from the main road. A dog barked just ahead, around a bend and Theo hoped the thing was leashed and friendly.

His mind turned to Avery, who had been friendly and pleasant, but not at all pushy like so many service workers can be as he worked behind the bar. Then later the man was cold and implacable as he stared down the mugger in the alley. Avery's posture and tone had been unmistakable, even though Theo hadn't been able to see his face. Once he turned back to Theo, he had once again been warm and open.

It was a dichotomy that made him uneasy, but still, when he considered it, Theo found nothing but the belief that Avery was exactly what he claimed: a man whose self-proclaimed purpose was to protect. A charming, hand-some warrior.

With that thought still on his mind, Theo stepped care-fully around the scraggly bush that blocked his view and came almost face to face with the dog he heard earlier– holy hell, *was* that a dog? The thing was huge and looked more like a damn wolf, but he couldn't imagine tame wolves were a real thing. The dog–Theo was going with dog–was with a couple of kids being glared down by none other than Marielle Trevor herself, in all her entitled fury. The older of the two kids couldn't be more than twelve and glared mutinously at the woman, putting his body between her and his younger brother, who seemed to be perhaps five or six.

The dog crowded the young boy's side, trying to provide comfort while also trying to put itself between the children and the blonde woman who was glaring at them furiously. Theo's skin prickled again–frankly, he was getting tired of the sensation–and he frowned at both the feeling and the scene in front of him.

"HOA regulations prohibit pets over twenty-five pounds. Your parents will be fined and that animal *will* be removed!"

The smaller of the children burst into sobs and buried his face in the animal's fur. The dog immediately tried to figure out how to continue standing guard and twist to lick the child's head at the same time. In a different situation Theo would have smiled at the scene.

Who did Marielle think she was, anyway? Ms. Almira Gulch confiscating Toto? Theo did try not to smirk now as the image of Marielle turning into the Wicked Witch of the West popped into his mind.

"And speaking of that, just where *are* your parents? Hmm? What are you doing out here on your own? That's neglect!" she said, not quite snarling but definitely not speaking kindly to the kids. "CPS should be alerted!"

"They're at home. They know where we are and there's no reason we can't be here!" the older child protested. "We're not doing anything wrong, and you can't get us in trouble!"

"I am the *president* of the *HOA* and an *adult*. *You* don't get to tell *me* if you're doing something wrong or not! Children are not allowed out here unsupervised. Now go home and I will call animal control to pick up that... that *thing*. I have the authority here so you'd better get moving!" The younger child wailed louder and the dog's ears finally swiveled back to lay against its head at the woman's tone.

"Actually, Marielle, we're all on county property right now. You don't have any authority here at all." Theo stepped forward. He wasn't sure why he was intervening other than basic decency and the desire to prevent an animal attack. There was no doubt that the dog–seriously, what breed of dog *was* that thing?–was fully aware that the woman was bullying and frightening the kids he belonged to, and was gearing up to protect them. "The HOA stops at the edge of our property lines."

"What?" Her head whipped up so she could see who dared interrupt her.

"I said that you have no particular authority here. Everything within fifteen feet of the river is county property. The estate lawyer went over it all in a lot of detail when I was signing the papers. This isn't part of the neighborhood, so it doesn't matter if you're the president of the HOA."

He wasn't about to point out that he had read the novels-worth of rules she gave him and there were no HOA regulations about kids playing unsupervised anyway. She would likely just call an emergency meeting and make a whole bunch of new rules up to fix that oversight, and he didn't want to be responsible for causing that.

Theo glanced at the kids who were watching him warily. The dog had settled slightly and was nudging the younger child with its head, trying to soothe the boy, who turned and wrapped both arms around the animal's neck in what had to be a strangling grip, but the dog just sat down and tried to lick the kid's ear.

"Theo! Out for a stroll on this lovely morning?" Marielle tried to smile at him, but it looked crooked and unpracticed. "I know it isn't *technically* part of the neighborhood, but it is in spirit, and it is my duty to ensure neighborhood standards are kept up!" She tried to smile at him again and sent him a look like she expected him to sympathize and agree.

"It really isn't." Theo wasn't going to play her game. He may not have much use for people in general anymore, but he wasn't about to let this wannabe socialite adult bully actual kids.

"If these children—and their parents"—she glared at the kids and narrowed her eyes at the dog—"refuse to comply I will have to levy a fine against them and call the authorities to remove the animal, as well as have someone come out here to do something about abandoned children."

Abandoned children? Was this woman for real?

"You do what you feel you have to do, Marielle." Theo shrugged. "I'll be happy to talk to the authorities as a witness when they arrive. Why don't you head on home and I'll handle the kids, okay? Off you go."

Theo wasn't sure where he found the patience to calmly herd her toward the path that cut between houses back to the sidewalk, but he managed somehow, and let out a sigh of relief when he heard a car door slam and the engine turn over. He stood there, staring back toward the street, even though he couldn't see her SUV, and waited until the engine noise faded into the background with the rest of the traffic.

A warm, furry head pushed itself into his hand and a heavy body shoved up against his leg. The wolf-dog leaned into him and bumped his hand again, and Theo swallowed his nerves to give the creature a scratch behind its massive ears.

What big ears you have, Grandmother! was all he could think.

"Do you think she's really gonna call the cops, mister?" The older kid stepped up beside him and peered up at his face, his arm wrapped around his brother's shoulders. The younger kid had stopped crying, but his bleary red eyes and wet face made it clear that he wasn't far from it.

"She might. People like that..." Theo bit back his words. These were kids, after all. "I'll stick around just in case. I think the only law that they might be able to enforce is the leash law if there is one. No laws against taking your, uh, your dog for a walk."

"He's not a dog, mister, he's—" The younger kid was cut off when the older one glared at him, then wrapped him up in another hug.

"Well, um. Whatever he is, then. Probably best to call him a dog if the police do show up." Theo wasn't entirely sure that was true, but he wasn't sure what else to say.

"Um. Do you live nearby? Ms. Trevor seemed to know you," the older boy asked

Theo nodded. "Yeah. I just moved here a few weeks ago. I live down that way, in the house with the picket fence."

"Oh! Mr. Garfield's house? We were pretty sad when he passed away. He was always nice to us when he saw us in the mornings," the older boy said. He stuck out his hand. "I'm Arturo Cardoso, but everyone calls me Artie. This is my brother Abe. Abelardo."

Theo solemnly shook Artie's hand. "Theobold Warren, but you can call me Theo."

"I didn't know that anyone bought Mr. Garfield's house," Artie said, cocking his head to the side. Theo stifled a grin when the wolf-dog did the exact same thing, sitting next to Abe again.

"I didn't buy it, actually. He was my great-uncle, and he left it to me in his will. I was a little surprised since I didn't know him very well, but I hope he can rest peacefully with his decision," Theo said. He wasn't sure why he was divulging this information to kids, but something about them seemed to draw the words out.

There must be something in the water, making him feel chattier than usual. First Avery, now these kids.

"Oh. That makes sense I guess. But he died a while ago." Artie nodded, but the wolf-dog seemed to study Theo for a long moment before whuffing and turning back to Abe to snuffle his nose into the child's belly, making him giggle.

"Yeah. I had things back in Nebraska that I was in the middle of. And I didn't hear about it until well after the funeral, so I couldn't even come pay my respects." By design, apparently. It had been a stipulation in Garfield's instructions to his lawyer.

Artie frowned for a moment then shrugged. "Anyway. We should go home, I guess. If Ms. Trevor calls the cops or whatever and they go to the house before we can warn them, our parents will freak out."

Theo nodded. "Mind if I walk with you? If she does send the cops this way I can fend them off better than you can. I don't know what the deal is if she calls animal control though." He grimaced and glanced at the dog.

"Oh, that's not a problem," Artie grinned up at him, mischief and secrets dancing in his eyes. "We don't have any pets."

"But..." Theo frowned and looked at the wolf-dog who he swore was grinning now. The dog stood and licked Abe's face, making the child laugh–which was a vastly better sound than the sobbing from a few minutes ago–and butted his head against Artie's belly. Artie scrubbed his fingers through the thick fur of the animal's neck and murmured something into the huge ear.

The dog then turned to Theo and regarded him for a moment before butting his head into Theo's hip in much the same way he had Artie, then turned and trotted off down the trail. If Theo hadn't known better he would have sworn the dog was saying goodbye and then heading off to his own home.

"What..."

"Come on, you can walk with us." Artie headed off down the trail in the other direction, back toward where Theo's house also lay. Abe stepped up to him with a grin and grabbed his hand, tugging him along the path.

"Um. Where..."

"Oh, he doesn't live with us," Artie said, throwing a grin over his shoulder. "He just came by to check up on us. He does that on the weekends, usually. He just came down the river from college. I guess traffic has been really weird lately so it was easier to walk."

"But..." Theo had no idea where to even start with that. "Check up on you?"

"Yeah. Mateo used to babysit us, but this year he's too busy most of the time, and he's all the way on campus. But he's kinda like a big brother so he worries." Artie shrugged and stomped up to the sidewalk.

Abe tried to run and catch up with his brother but tripped over a stray weed. Theo reached out by instinct and caught him before he landed while his brain was still trying to process everything. That monster dog–and he was absolutely not going to consider any other option there, certainly not that it was a real wolf here in the suburbs– was like a *big brother?* Theo had heard of animals getting protective of their humans, especially of the children, so that wasn't too much of a stretch, but this seemed...

And that *dog* babysat them? On what planet was that a thing that made sense? And now it was at *college?*

"Arturo? Who is this?"

Theo was shaken out of his thoughts by a woman's voice.

"Mama, this is Mr. Theo. He lives in Mr. Garfield's house," Abe said, bounding up the front walk. "He saved us and Mateo from the mean lady!"

"He what now?" the woman asked, swooping Abe up into her arms and blowing a raspberry on his neck to make him giggle. She glanced over his shoulder at Artie for more detail.

"Ms. Trevor found us when we were hanging out with Mateo by the river, and started yelling about animal control and stuff. Mr. Theo told her that the river is county property and she can't do anything about it and she got really mad and stormed off."

"That woman," she said in a tone very similar to Ivette's, her eyes blazing. "Thank you, Mr. Theo." She put Abe down and held a hand out. "Stacy Cardoso, thanks for the help. That woman has been doing her level best to drive out all the older residents, and a few of the new ones, since she got here. Getting herself elected as HOA president was, apparently, exactly the leverage she needed to throw her weight around."

"Theobold Warren, but you can just call me Theo," he said for the second time that morning, shaking her hand. He had to blink at her bright copper hair and jade-green eyes, incongruous next to the boys' darker coloring.

"Oh, your face!" Stacy laughed, but the sound wasn't rude at all. It made him feel like he was in on the joke.

"I bet I can guess what's making you look so determined not to say something," she continued. "They take after my husband in pretty much all ways. My family's very Irish, but Jorge's genetics definitely won the coin toss with the boys." She shrugged, with a smile. "I'm sorry if you have incurred the wrath of Marielle for being a decent human being."

"Anyone eager to pick on kids isn't someone I want to associate much with anyway," Theo said. Between the mugging, and both interactions with Marielle, and the texts from his mother, he was already nearing his limit for people for the weekend. The strange interactions were just exhausting and he had been having a lot of them lately.a

Stacy grinned and shooed the kids inside. "Well, good luck. And welcome to the neighborhood. We miss Garfield, but it's very good to meet you."

"Thanks. I didn't know him well, but I'm glad he thought of me. It's nice here," Theo said. Then he huffed a small laugh and shook his head. "Well, except for Marielle."

Stacy laughed all the way into the house after her kids, and Theo let out a breath of relief.

7

ACCUSATIONS

"Then he asked if I was available to teach and I figured I could make the time. So, I started teaching self-defense at the college gym too, twice a week. Between that, my normal classes, and my work here, I stay pretty busy." Avery leaned his elbow on the bar top. The regular bartender walked past and dropped a bottle of water next to him, and took away Avery's plate with just a few polite words.

Theo had tried to stay in bed that morning, but his mind kept replaying the last few days on a loop. His mom's calls and texts. Getting assaulted by that mugger. Getting rescued. Marielle harassing those kids. It was exhausting and more social than he'd been in weeks. The mental squirrels just kept running in circles until he couldn't take it. He had to get out and distract himself somehow, which is how he found himself back at the Three-Legged Wolf, eating another burger.

To be fair, they had really good burgers.

Avery came to sit with him about halfway through his late lunch and ordered something himself. He told Theo that he had been teaching classes all morning and wanted some real food before he set himself up at the door for the evening. At least it was Sunday and most of the college kids were sleeping off hangovers, so it didn't much matter that Avery was a bit tired. Theo ducked questions about his book, so Avery took up the conversational slack by explaining his life's work.

"And you get to feel like you're keeping people safe," Theo said, remembering their previous conversation. Avery nodded.

"Yeah. The self-defense classes really help me feel like—"

"There he is."

Avery's face went blank, his posture shifting slightly, and Theo suddenly got an idea of what his face must have looked like to the mugger. The cheerful, puckish young man was gone, again instantly replaced by a resolute warrior. There was something... *other* about the man, though. *A fae warrior*, Theo decided. *Though one who is standing guard rather than engaging an enemy. And where the hell are all these fanciful thoughts coming from?*

He turned to face whoever it was that stood behind him, apparently looking for him, and find out what she wanted. A petite brunette woman stood there with her arms crossed and a glare firmly on her face. She looked like she had eaten something nasty, and Theo had served it to her.

Beside her was a man who to Theo's eye screamed "cop" even though he was wearing designer jeans and a soft green T-shirt under a blazer, all expensive brands, if he wasn't mistaken. Theo was immediately put off by the man, who seemed far too similar to the very people who had stabbed him in the back in Nebraska and sent him running here in the first place. Avery stood and faced the pair.

"Something I can help you with, Officer?" Avery asked. "I may be on my break, but I do work here."

The edge in his voice made the hair on the back of Theo's neck stand up.

The cop raised his hands in a placating gesture. "I'm not here to stir anything up. I'm Detective Robert Angelo and I'm investigating the rash of tagging that's cropped up lately." He reached into his jacket and pulled out a silver card case, handing one to each of them. "I was hoping that I could ask Mr. Warren a few questions. I'm very curious about the area, and I hope you can fill in some gaps, since you've had family here for so long."

"I barely knew my great-uncle. And what could you possibly think that I could tell you?" Theo asked, blinking. "I just moved here, and all I can tell you about it is that I got mugged near some creepy spray painted tag the other day."

"Ms. Baxter caught up to me just a minute ago and pointed out that you are new to the area. New people see things a bit differently, notice different things than those of us who've been around for a while. I was hoping we could talk and maybe you could give me some insight." Detective Angelo put his card case away and smiled. It was so blatantly his "good-cop" smile that Theo felt his own eyes narrow in response.

"And that's why Candace dragged you in here all smug like she's got the upper hand somehow?" Avery asked, completely deadpan.

"I am honestly not sure why Ms. Baxter is still here. She saw me walking down the sidewalk"–Detective Angelo's eyes started to slide toward the woman, who was almost vibrating with outrage at being ignored then discussed like she wasn't there–"and she suggested that I come in and talk to Mr. Warren due to the reasoning I just mentioned. Maybe we could find someplace quiet to talk?"

Theo tried not to twitch. Detective Angelo did make a good point: it was entirely likely that Theo saw things completely differently than the people who had lived here for years. People got used to things, stopped actively noticing when the neighbor's dog was barking at the mailman every day or that the traffic at that stoplight was always terrible. It became the background noise of life. But to Theo, it was all fresh and noticeable. And it was, after all, the man's job to ask questions.

Still. There was a note in the detective's voice that seemed just-so-slightly off. The false friendliness and the smarmy smile were itching under Theo's skin. His tone was friendly on the surface, but he was putting more than a touch of cop authority behind it, making it seem like the polite words were more social niceties than an actual option to turn him down.

Or maybe Theo was just hearing what he expected to hear. It sure seemed as if the man was willing to be swayed by whatever heresay he came across if the way he was taking this Candace woman seriously. And all that put him decidedly on Theo's wrong side right now.

"It all started when he moved here!" her attitude finally exploded out of her mouth, uncontainable by her slight body any longer. "He must have something to do with it, there's no other explanation! There was no graffiti anywhere before that, he brought the hoodlums into our quiet neighborhood." She sneered at Theo and he felt his eyebrows creep up his forehead.

"You have got to be joking," he shot back, unable to stay quiet any longer. "You think I have something to do with graffiti because I *moved in?*"

"You come creeping in here like you own the place–" Candace screeched, but Theo wasn't having it.

"If you mean my house, then I do, in fact, own the place. If you want to call and ask my lawyer about it you're welcome to do so." Theo's temper flared.

"Sir," Detective Angelo cut in, trying to take control of the situation. "I really do just want to ask a couple of questions. If you've seen anything unusual. That's all." His tone was firm, but again, suggestive that Theo did not, in fact, have much of a choice.

Theo knew damn well he did.

"I've spoken to Marielle Trevor," Angelo said, eyeing Avery's hair and piercings. "She seemed sure that someone in the neighborhood knows something about these vandals. She's very concerned about a criminal element coming into the area."

"A criminal element?" Theo snorted. "Does she mean me? Oh yes, I'm extremely dangerous. I'll get you all messed up on science reporting."

"I don't believe that she meant you, particularly," Angelo said. "But perhaps you're not aware of all the facts of some of your neighbors. It would be very helpful if you could confirm some things for me." His gaze flicked back to Avery for just a second, but Theo caught it. It seemed that the detective's eyes were the thing to watch.

"I have to tell you two things, Detective. First, I have no information for you about the vandalism other than it's messy. Second, I am not a fan of either bullies or bigots."

Avery had caught the glance too.

"I may not be a lawyer, but I think I should advise Mr. Warren not to answer a damn thing unless you're a bit more forthcoming as to why you need to talk to him, specifically," Avery cut in. "Not to mention–"

"This has nothing to do with you, you degenerate

punk," the brunette started, but the detective raised a hand to stop her before she worked up into a full rant.

"Ms. Baxter–"

"I won't stand around and let chaotic elements destroy my community!" Candace huffed.

"And you are making a scene. I'm going to have to ask you to leave, Candace, until you can calm down and behave yourself," Avery said, his tone leaving no room for argument.

"I have a right to be here, this is a public place! You can't make me leave!"

Was this woman serious? Theo sighed. Of course, she was.

"Actually, I can. This may a public place, but it is also a private establishment and I am in charge of security here. If you do not leave on your own, I will escort you out, and if you continue harassing our customers I will be forced to call the police."

"Hah!" Candace was smug now. "I have the police here with me! You can't do anything about it!"

"I'm sure that the detective would be the first to tell you that you storming in here with a cop in tow would have absolutely no effect on your ejection from this place of business. Now since you are apparently not willing to leave on your own I will have to escort you out." Avery stepped forward, planting himself between Theo and the pair.

"I am asking one last time, Candace. Leave now on your own or I will take you outside myself." Avery spoke calmly and clearly, and Theo could see the moment the woman realized she wasn't going to win this skirmish. Detective Angelo watched silently, taking in every detail of the exchange.

"Come on, Detective," Candace huffed. "I'll tell you

everything you need to know, then you can do your job and clean up this town." She spun on her heel and stormed off.

"I had probably better go calm her down," Detective Angelo grimaced, conceding that he had completely lost control of the moment. "I'm sorry about that. But please, give me a call so we can talk, Mr. Warren. I'd like to hear your thoughts."

"Other than finding traffic in the area entirely inexplicable I have no *thoughts*, in particular, to share with you, Detective." Theo wasn't about to let some strange woman have him arrested for whatever grudge she had against him for inheriting a house.

Detective Angelo sent him a hard look but nodded before heading out the door after Candace. The few patrons who had been pretending not to watch turned back to their meals. Avery frowned at the door and with a visible effort, shook off the heavy mood before turning back to Theo.

"Marielle's minions are just such a joy." Avery smiled, but the expression was a bit flat. Nowhere near the easy good humor from just a few minutes ago.

"Marielle's minions?"

"Candace is on the HOA board."

"Ah." Theo wasn't sure how else to respond, so he just nodded.

"Wait here a sec." Avery sighed and headed to the door to the back, to disappear for a few minutes. When he came back he was much closer to his previous mood.

"Boss has been alerted to her shenanigans and he said to comp your lunch. Wish he'd just ban those obnoxious women, but this is the most active trouble any of them have caused, so..." He shrugged and picked up a bar towel, flicking it over his shoulder.

"That's not necessary, but thanks." He couldn't think of

anything else to say. Still, his mouth opened and he said, "Degenerate?"

Avery rolled his eyes. "Those HOA folk have it in their heads that Darren and I are having some sort of kinky sex fest at home. Because apparently they can't conceive of cousins living together as adults."

"They think you're sleeping with your cousin?" Theo blinked.

Avery glanced up at the door she had left through, then over at the stools the women had been sitting on earlier. He sent Theo a long stare that seemed to be looking right into his soul, looking for something. Theo had to stop himself from fidgeting under that gaze, and vaguely hoped he didn't disappoint the other man.

After a long moment, Avery seemed to shrug with his whole body. "Marielle and her people don't like anything that gets in the way of their perfect ideal utopia of blandness. They like things to be clean, orderly, magazine-spread-perfect at all times. Then there's those of us that are..." Avery glanced down at himself, looking for the right words.

"Colorful?" Theo offered, glancing at Avery's hair.

Avery chuckled. "That's a good word. Yeah." He drove his fingers through his aqua curls and rubbed the back of his neck. "Anyway. Darren moved here a few years before she did. Before the development was finished and they formed the HOA. I moved in a few years after, right after Marielle got herself onto the HOA board. I had just graduated high school and had the final confrontation with my dad. She took one look at my hair and my skinny teenage fashion statements and decided I was a troublemaker. Then she saw me out in town, on a date with a *man*, and she started in with the wild sexual innuendo." Avery grimaced and glanced away from Theo.

Theo blinked. "She's homophobic?"

"She's anything that's not in her perfect image of American Suburbia-phobic. So, yeah." Avery rolled his eyes. "A lot of the people who moved into the new houses are very much like her. Upper middle class. Soccer-mom styled. White. You know the drill. But the 'degenerate' bit? She saw me and Darren hug once, which is obviously code for 'we have sex,' right? So now she's convinced we're sleeping together and having orgies on the side. Or, not on the side. Whatever."

Theo blinked at him. "You can't be serious."

Avery leveled his gaze back at Theo. "I could not possibly make that up. And I think we look enough alike that it's obvious we're related somehow, so..."

"Deviant. Got it." Theo shook his head. "That's insane. That woman..."

"Yeah. The older residents didn't care too much for the new houses but didn't realize what an active pain in the ass the new HOA would be. The developer sold everyone on the idea because they were building a park and tennis courts and stuff over by the footbridge, and hoped that everyone paying into an HOA to maintain it all would "foster a sense of community" according to the literature I turned up when I cleaned out the den a while back and found the paperwork. Darren has the bad habit of squirreling away papers he doesn't need away wherever he is at the time and forgetting about them completely."

"Ugh. So the older residents didn't really attend any setup meetings, nor did they really think about the HOA until it was all a done deal." Theo picked up the narrative and drew the conclusion out of the mess. "And now everyone's stuck. I got it. That's awful."

"Pretty much. The older folk don't understand it at all, and a lot of the younger ones don't have the courage to stand up to the woman. Those of us in the older homes are all grandfathered out of a lot of the HOA rules since the developer who set it all up wasn't actively evil, just short-sighted and stupid, so folk just sort of keep their heads down and try to ignore Marielle when she blusters around."

Theo nodded. "I got it. That explains why she was so angry I stepped in when she was harassing those kids. They were just playing down by the river with some giant wolf-dog, not doing anyone any harm or making any trouble. I happened to be there and pointed out that the county land is out of her jurisdiction and that I didn't think that *kids playing outside* was against the law."

Avery threw back his head and laughed, the sound dancing around the bar like rainbows thrown off a prism. "Oh, I bet that made you an enemy for sure. You were already starting from behind a bit, I bet, what with Garfield's research and all that. Unless you've cleared everything out of the house, anyway. She's been foaming at the mouth to get in there and see what he was doing, and you don't seem like the sort to let her in to rummage around."

"His research?" Theo thought of the towers of books and the papers stuffed into cubbies in the room that had very obviously been his great-uncle's office.

"Lord. He and Darren used to get into the most mind-numbing conversations about the history of the area. Their research overlapped enough to bore everyone around them to tears when they got onto it. Darren's applied for a grant to dig even deeper into local pre-settler history, and keeps going on about it at *great* length" Avery rolled his eyes again, then groaned. "Ugh. I suppose I ought to go actually clock in if I'm pulling the 'I am security' card. It's pretty close to my shift anyway."

Avery grabbed his plate and when Theo nodded, took his as well before he hustled off through the door to the back. Once the man was out of sight, Theo leaned on his elbows and stared at his half-finished beer. Why on earth would a self-absorbed jerk so focused on appearances as Marielle want anything to do with an old man's nutty research? Or maybe she just wanted to snoop around in general. That seemed more likely.

And what sort of research would overlap local history, fairy tales, and—as far as Theo could tell—random bits of junk? Every room except the dining room and the kitchen was stuffed with bits and pieces of what he could only think of as his uncle's magpie collection: broken watches, crystals, twigs tied together with vines or thread, and pressed flowers in books. Old coins and bigger stones and some seashells. All sorts of odd things.

And, like Avery's cousin apparently, papers were stuffed in all sorts of places. Theo had spent his first day in the house clearing out the dining room and some of the kitchen so he could work there. The light was cheerful in there and it was already the tidiest, so he had set up in there and not really worried about the rest of it.

He hadn't even cleared out Great-uncle's room, instead sleeping in a guest room that wasn't too full of stuff.

"You look like a man deep in thought." Avery's voice startled him.

"Oh, just letting my mind wander, you know. I should head off. All this excitement is exhausting after the last few days. I think I'm worn out."

Avery chuckled. "That's fair. Go get some rest, man. And don't be a stranger!"

"You bet." Theo nodded his thanks, snatched up his bag, and fled.

8

THE LAST POT

Theo stood just outside the Wolf, stumped now as to what he should do. He had taken two hours to eat his lunch and was somewhat hungry again already. Maybe for a snack, but as he mentally reviewed the groceries in his kitchen, he groaned. He didn't want to go back into the pub, wasn't sure what to say to Avery or anyone else inside after that scene with the detective and the HOA woman, but he also didn't want to go home.

So much for moving somewhere new, where nobody knew him and he could just fade into the background and not be bothered.

Theo stood on what he had started thinking of as "downtown main street" even though it was neither downtown nor a main street. Just down from the Three-Legged Wolf was the secondhand shop that he still needed to visit, and past that a bunch of other shops lined the street, beckoning him with their windows. Who knew what sort of treasures were out there?

At least there must be somewhere to get a decent cup of coffee.

There were craft shops and a boutique clothing store that definitely catered to the Marielle Trevors of the world. Just as Theo hoped he wouldn't have to go much farther for his treat, he spotted a sign for the Last Pot Cafe.

The chalkboard propped outside said in loopy letters "Let this be a sign that you need a coffee break" with a drawing of a steaming cup of coffee below it, and Theo decided he would go in anyway. If the coffee was good enough to rise above the cute-quote-signboard trend, he could forgive a multitude of marketing sins. A sign in the corner of the front window said they were hiring.

He shivered as he reached for the door handle, something making him pause for a moment. It wasn't anything he could really explain, just a sense of place, perhaps, or of rightness. Whatever it was, he shook it off and stepped into the surprisingly airy space anyway, determined to explore his new town. Pale mint walls set off the mural on the left side that felt for all the world like you could follow the painted path under the ancient trees and meet a fae prince just around the bend who would whisk you off on adventures. He thought again of Avery, who would fit perfectly into the slightly magical scene on the wall.

Theo blinked away the odd thought, then shrugged and decided he liked the place. He *had* to get a handle on these fanciful daydreams. Yes, the man was cute, but Theo wasn't here to flirt with anyone, nor did he have time to waste on impractical, unscientific nonsense. His mother would be appalled to know how much time he had wasted over the last few days on that sort of intellectually empty foolishness.

It wasn't busy in the shop, and the barista at the end of the counter was scowling vaguely out the window, but the man behind the register was smiling brightly.

"Welcome to the Last Pot Cafe, do you want a table or are you ordering to go?" he asked when Theo stepped close to the counter.

"Um, to go, I suppose," Theo answered, then thought better of it. "No, wait. I'll stay for a bit. You have food, and I ought to eat something that might qualify as healthy today."

The barista chuckled. "One of those days, huh? Well, what floats your fancy? Are you a fancy coffee and complicated order type or a no-nonsense need-to-fuel-up kind of guy? We've got some pretty good offerings either way."

Theo debated the question, and as he was the only one in line, he took his time. "I think I'm a no-nonsense coffee sort today, but I'm also stalling somewhat before getting back home. So perhaps a complicated meal order."

The barista laughed, and Theo found himself relaxing a bit. The tension he had carried since the interaction with the snippy brunette started seeping out of his shoulders.

"Well, we have a really nice vegetable-stuffed Portobello with an autumn harvest soup today, if you're willing to eat vegetables, served with a really fantastic rustic bread. I can also recommend the bacon cranberry panini. It sounds a little odd, but it's really good."

"Hmm. Think I can get the first suggestion to eat here and the sandwich to go when I leave? And a latte."

"I like your style, man. Why choose?" The barista laughed again and rang him up. "You in town for business or just passing through?"

"Just moved here a few weeks ago, actually. I'm still getting my bearings," Theo said. He wasn't sure why he was volunteering the information, but somehow the combination of the whimsical decor and the cheerful fellow behind the counter was disarming.

"Oh! Welcome to Whitelake!"

"Thanks." Theo paid and dropped his change in the tip jar.

"Grab a table anywhere you want. The weird traffic lately is scaring folks off a bit, and the mugging down the block."

"Mugging?" Theo stopped turning to look back at the young man.

"Yeah." The barista looked sad for a moment, then shrugged. "I don't really know much about it and I won't repeat gossip, but a woman was mugged last week. Some thug yanked her into the ally down the block and was super rough. I saw a couple of the bruises under her makeup when she came in yesterday morning, telling some wild stories to her friends. But this isn't a dangerous area, so don't worry. That's the first incident I've heard of in years, aside from the graffiti. We got tagged this morning, even! The owner has some guys coming to clean it off in about an hour."

"Well, I hope she's all right. That must have been scary." Theo had no idea what to say to any of that. He had no desire to talk abou this own experience, thank you very much. "And your wall, I guess, too. I hope the paint came off it okay."

Part of him was horrified that someone else had been targeted, but a little gremlin in the back of his mind whispered that at least he wasn't the only one. There was even a small part of him that felt embarrassed by what happened, though his rational mind knew that was ridiculous. He even had a faint memory of Marielle mentioning a mugging back when she handed off the tome of HOA rules.

Not sure what made him think that he had been

singled out the other night, he frowned and made an appropriately sympathetic sound.

"Yeah. I figure that as long as we all stick together it'll be fine. This place is usually so safe that any little bit of crime feels like the end of the world, you know? This whole town is charmed, it seems like, but especially over here near the park," he chattered on, unaware of the nerve he'd hit with the little bit of gossip. "I'm sure it'll all clear up soon. Seems to be the way of things here, which is nice. I'll bring your food out to you in a few minutes."

Theo wandered over to a table and sat, pulling his phone from his pocket to poke at as he waited, but found himself staring out the window at the cars slowly rolling by.

"God, it's been like that all day. Why are we even here for this?" the grumpy barista grumbled as she turned to make his drink.

"Gotta pay the bills, right?" the cheerful one answered. "The morning rush was about normal, and tomorrow will pick up again. You know how it goes. And if it was busy you'd just complain about Manny leaving next week." Theo could practically hear the shrug.

"I hate being bored, and there's only so many times I can clean shit around here," she groused. The machine whirring to life cut off any more of the conversation.

Outside, someone stopped to look at the help-wanted sign and Theo glanced over to see the young blond boy he had seen across the river the other day. There was no sign of the older, angry-looking one, and Theo found himself relieved.

The young man frowned at the sign, then peered through the window at the shop. His gaze met Theo's for a moment and the blond's eyes widened for a moment before he dropped his gaze and hurried away. A tray of cups rattled behind him.

"There you go. Hope it lives up to my recommendation!"

"Smells great," Theo startled, his attention snapping back to the present. He nodded his thanks to the chipper barista and picked up his fork.

"Enjoy your meal! I'll bring your to-go box in a bit."

Theo found himself smiling back at the man and nodded again before he tucked into the food and closed his eyes to savor his first bite. Warm and comforting, the pumpkin and sweet potato flavors melted into each other and whatever spices were used brought the whole bowl to life. Theo could easily see himself taking this home with him and settling in front of a fire with his lunch and a good book. It was the cafe lunch version of a snuggly blanket.

Oh yeah. He would definitely be back.

———

Theo was just walking up to his house, full of soup and stuffed mushroom and feeling surprisingly content with life when he noticed someone standing on his porch. A man stood by his front door in tan slacks and a blue button-up shirt, like he had just escaped his office. He turned and smiled as he looked curiously at the cat in the chair, a covered Tupperware dish in his hands.

"Hello?" Theo called as he approached. "Sorry, I was out, can I help you?"

The man's pine-bark-brown eyes crinkled at the corners when he smiled, the warmth in them feeling a bit like sitting in the sun under a tree on a perfect early summer day.

"Hello, Theo Warren?" the man's voice matched his eyes, warm and pleasant.

"Yes?" Apparently, this entire conversation was going to be conducted via questions.

"I am Jorge Cardoso. You saved my sons from the clutches of the terrible Marielle yesterday."

"Oh," Theo said. He blinked and shifted slightly. "I don't know that I would go quite that far, but I was happy to help out. She must have needed more coffee before leaving her house or something."

Jorge chuckled. "Probably." His smile dimmed a bit. "She is very eager to find any excuse she can to harass some of us. The older residents, you know. The... not-like-her residents. My family has lived in this area for generations, and many of us still have homes here in this neighborhood. You have met your neighbor Ivette?" He nodded at the house next door.

"Yeah?" Theo was back to questions.

"My second cousin." Jorge grinned. "We're everywhere."

Theo couldn't stop his own grin from trying to match Jorge's. He stepped up to the door and held out a hand which Jorge shook.

"At any rate, Stacy sent me here with these as a thank-you and welcome to the neighborhood. I wish I had been there when you came by, but I've been stuck in meetings all week." Jorge rolled his eyes then smiled. "Anyway, if we had known Garfield had family coming we would have come to introduce ourselves earlier. We had no idea. Do you plan to carry on his work?"

Theo frowned slightly. "I barely knew the guy, to be honest. I was shocked when I got the call about the will and wasn't sure what to do about it, but then I had to move suddenly and here I am. If I find out what his work was maybe I'll look into it, though."

For some reason, he didn't want to disappoint this man. Maybe it was just the warm feeling of family and *belonging* that the man exuded. He was like some sort of archetypical uncle, the one you liked to sit next to at family functions because he wouldn't ask stupid, prying questions or irritate you.

"Well, it would be nice to see if anything came of it. He was not a straightforward man, but he was a determined one," Jorge said. "At any rate, Stacy and the boys and I are grateful that you stepped in. Thank you." He handed the box to Theo, who felt the warmth through the plastic. "Mateo is happy to know you're here and friendly, as well."

"I'm glad I was there. I'm not fond of screeching bullies." He'd had enough of that with Penny at the end. And how would this man know the thoughts of a wol–a dog?

Jorge chuckled again. "She is that more often than not, true. She has redeeming qualities, though, I am sure of it, but I suppose she is on the warpath now. You didn't immediately fall in line with what she thinks you should be, therefore you must be one of the 'riffraff' as she calls the rest of us."

Theo groaned. "I kind of guessed that when her minion tried to have me arrested for vandalism."

Jorge's face fell. "She didn't."

"She did. They decided that since the tagging started around the time I got here, that obviously makes me the vandal."

"Well, you must admit it's quite a coincidence." A new voice startled them and Theo fumbled the box of brownies, barely saving the precious cargo. He looked up and sighed at the man who stood on the path approaching his porch.

"Detective. Is there something I can do for you?"

Detective Angelo looked up at him steadily and Theo wondered if he did that to make people fidget and be less careful. Mostly it just annoyed the hell out of Theo, and Candace's smugly satisfied face as she threw out her accusation flashed in his mind. That's two snide, arrogant women he'd had to deal with this week, and he'd had enough. Theo wasn't about to be bullied into anything, even if they had the entire police force pandering to them.

"Well, I was hoping to talk to you, since we no longer run the risk of Ms. Baxter causing a scene and being thrown out of a bar." The detective's tone was so dry that Theo was surprised cactuses didn't spring up in his yard.

"Candace got tossed out of the Wolf?" Jorge's eyes were bright with laughter. "Oh, I wish I'd been there to see that! I bet Avery felt very satisfied."

"Oh?" Detective Angelo smiled at the man and raised his eyebrows like he was looking for a good bit of gossip.

Jorge peered down at the detective, his lips pursed and expression wary for a moment before answering.

"Oh, they have been after Avery for years now. Marielle doesn't care for anyone who doesn't kowtow to her great and powerful status as HOA president." He shrugged as if it was nothing very interesting, but his eyes were sharp and watchful.

Something about the statement felt incomplete, and the sudden thought that his neighbors knew more about... *something* than they were saying slammed into Theo's brain.

"Yeah, I did get that impression," Angelo agreed with a sigh. "Look, I am sorry about the scene from earlier Mr. Warren. Ms. Baxter told me she knew someone who had information but didn't explain until we got there, and by then she was storming into the bar. I had no intentions of causing a scene like that."

"Yes, well. I'm sure she did. Again, I don't know anything about the vandalism, so there you go." Theo was tired of having his day interrupted by this nonsense. Once was bad enough, but twice? "I was, however mugged recently. Any luck on that case?"

"Mugged? I'll look into it," Angelo said without missing a beat. Theo had no doubt the detective knew all about it already. "But you did move here just as the vandal started up, is that right?"

"I haven't the faintest idea." Theo rather suspected that the man knew that too. Theo certainly had no clue as to the vandalism timeline. "If you'd like to know the history of the occupancy of this house, you're welcome to contact the estate lawyer. Otherwise, I suspect the person who thought to suggest to you that I have anything at all to do with it in the first place is only trying to use you to make a point: her way or the highway. If, as it seems, you are willing to base your investigation on rumors and malicious gossip, then I have nothing to discuss with you. In fact, since you are basing your interest in me on a foundation of malicious gossip, I think Avery had an excellent point. If you want to talk to me, you can call my lawyer," Theo said, as calmly as he could manage. He made a show of pulling out his keys and opening the lock.

"I don't know that we need to get that formal," Detective Angelo said. He stuffed his hands in his pockets and tried to look casual, but Theo could only see the designer labels that were no doubt sewn to every item of the detective's clothing. Too damn much like his ex-business partner. And his ex-girlfriend. And his current HOA president, dammit.

"Maybe we could just sit down and have a cup of coffee and sort this all out?" Angelo said.

"I've had a cup of coffee," Theo said, holding up the to-go bag that had the Last Pot's logo clearly stamped on it.

"Some tea, then?" the detective asked. His words and posture were friendly but his tone was growing harder and more determined. "I would really like to talk to you."

"I'm pretty sure Theo was trying to politely ask you to leave, Officer," Jorge stepped in. The warm, welcoming man that had handed Theo brownies had gone and was replaced by a man more implacable and solid. This man was not moving unless made to.

"There's no need to be aggressive sir," Detective Angelo started.

"Nobody's being aggressive here, Detective. You, however, are being rather pushy, and it sounds like you have no real reason for it. I thought that detectives were required to base their deductions on evidence and not hearsay?" Theo was over this conversation.

"That's true, but we get that evidence by listening to people. I never know when someone is going to say something important," Angelo said, his body language relaxed, but his eyes sharp. "And there is something very odd going on in this neighborhood."

"Yes, there is. There is a detective who is not noticing the clue that I am showing him that his welcome has run out. Now if you'll excuse us, my *friend* and I were about to have some brownies. Jorge?" Theo stepped back and let his new friend inside, then stepped back and closed the door in Detective Angelo's irritated face.

"Well, I guess I'm making coffee after all. Need something with those brownies." Theo sighed. "Sorry about that."

Jorge damn near sparkled with mirth. "Not at all.

Watching you put that man in his place was worth the adjustment to my schedule. And I will always make time for my wife's baking. She had to promise she'd make more to ensure I wouldn't eat the whole box before I got here."

Theo had to chuckle at that. "Well, they made it here safe and sound. I think that deserves a reward, don't you?"

"I knew I would like you, Theo." Jorge grinned widely and Theo laughed all the way to the kitchen.

9

CLEANUP

Theo was not in a great mood. The last few days had been just this side of insane.

Sunday afternoon, he went home from the bar understandably confused, not only by Avery and his odd determination to protect Theo from, well, everything, but also by the strange woman's sudden insistence that he had something to do with the tagging that was plaguing the area. Was she planning on accusing him of mugging himself too? His mind was already unsettled and he felt restless, and when his mother called to continue the discussion about her running into Penny, which was the last thing Theo wanted to do, he gave up on the rest of his day.

Why his mother was so hung up on his ex, Theo had no idea. She hadn't much cared for Penny until they'd broken up, and then suddenly Penny was the One That Got Away, even though Mom always had some comment about Penny's attitude or her unwillingness to stay in the workplace once she moved in with Theo. Never mind the fact that Penny cheated on him for at least a year. And never mind that the one thing that Theo really demanded was honesty and his mother knew that, and she *knew* that Penny had cheated on him.

He sighed and snarled at himself and stomped out to the garden shed to see what kind of mess the man he had started thinking of as Grunkle Garfield had left out there. If it was anything like the house it would be a magpie's nest. Probably stuffed full to bursting with crap, and Theo figured he'd be lucky if it didn't come pouring out of the door the moment he pulled on it like a thwarted cartoon child's attempt at cleaning their room by piling everything in the closet.

The cat stared at him disdainfully from a patch of garden sunshine as he threw the doors open and stopped. The shed was shockingly immaculate. Nothing at all like the house, with lord-only-knew what stuffed into any available corner. There were the usual yard care devices—a small lawnmower, a hedge trimmer, a rake, all that—neatly put away to the side of the small building.

The floor was swept, and the few hand tools inside were tidily hung on hooks on a pegboard over a small potting bench that had a few miscellaneous objects that seemed to be required in any garden shed: pots and trays and so on. One small cardboard box sat in the back, a neatly folded tarp sitting on top with what looked incongruously like the edge of a sleeping bag peeking from underneath, though Theo couldn't connect what he knew of Garfield to camping gear.

It looked for all the world like someone had just cleaned up.

The shed even *smelled* tidy, somehow, like just good, clean earth and a little motor oil scent from the lawnmower.

Weird. Well, maybe Grunkle's yard service had kept it tidy. Theo sighed and glanced around the yard. The lawyer had given him the name of the service they had used to keep the property up. Or take up Jorge's offer of Artie for lawn-mowing. Lord knew he wasn't going to be any use at the chore.

Shaking his head, he closed the door and headed back inside. The surprise had taken the edge off his irritation, but he was still restless. Welp. Might as well start in his own room, then, right? It wasn't as bad as most of the rest of the house, for some reason. Maybe Grunkle realized that any guests he might have wouldn't appreciate being buried under a mountain of random crap.

More likely, the man just hadn't gone in there often. Theo grabbed a garbage bag and trudged upstairs.

As he sorted through the pebbles and feathers and bits of twisted wood–put in a box to be taken outside rather than tossed in the garbage–and the books and papers– stacked on the bed to be taken to more appropriate locations or given away–Theo turned over in his mind what his life had become over the past few months.

Just under a year ago, he had been contentedly ignorant of the betrayals and the drama looming on the horizon. He had a girlfriend he lived with and planned to propose to since that was the next reasonable step in their relationship. He was a mostly silent partner in a small but fairly successful local chain of restaurants. His family was close by, he had a nice apartment, and he had a job he was good at even if the stuff he wrote about didn't exactly make him shiver with excitement. Usually.

Then the call from the lawyers. Great-uncle Garfield had died and left Theo everything. Well, almost every-thing. There were a few bequests to people Theo assumed were close friends or other relatives. He remembered sitting at his desk, stunned when the attorney had told him how much Theo was now worth. It didn't make a lick of sense that this man Theo had met once as a child had left so much to him.

Penny found him still sitting there an hour later, staring out the window at the back of the apartment building behind theirs as the sun set, turning the bricks in the wall a glowing red. She turned on the light, walked over to plop down in his lap, her arms snaking around his shoulders, and asked him what was wrong. So he told her, and unknowingly signed the death warrant on his whole life in Omaha.

Over the following months, Penny got increasingly vocal about selling the "dusty old mausoleum" even though she had never even been to Oregon, let alone in the house. She wanted to buy something new, fancy, and expensive in Omaha. A house, a mansion there in town where they could hold fancy parties. Someplace with a pool so she could have her friends over in the summer and sit next to it and have drinks and gossip. She always said the last bit with a grin, like she was teasing, but Theo had known her long enough that he could tell that she meant it all.

Something in Theo's soul had objected to the idea of just instructing the estate lawyers to liquidate everything. He at least wanted to come out and see it all again, one last time. Turned out to be a good thing he didn't let her talk him into selling. He needed a place to land when their relationship finally exploded so spectacularly.

This place was much better than the mess he had left behind. Even with the crazy HOA people and the insane rules they expected him to follow and the bizarre accusations Candace had thrown at him. Even with the mugging. Even with the local pub with the friendly punk bouncer-slash-bartender making him feel all social again when he didn't want to. This was where he would stay, pottering around on his own until he, too, died and passed the place on to some random relative.

Theo growled to himself and tossed another old book onto his bed, groaning when he saw the puff of dust that rose from it in response and covered his blankets. Fantastic. Now he had to do laundry or risk sneezing all damn night. Theo glanced around the room and decided that he'd cleared out enough for the moment. The closet was empty, and the dresser and windowsills no longer sported the eclectic collections. He could tackle the shelves later.

There was a bowl of coins from all over the world on the nightstand that he wasn't sure what to do with, and the box of what he was thinking of as "hiking mementos" to take down to the river or somewhere. And the books. What he'd do with all of Grunkle's books that had once resided under the bed or in the closet, Theo had no idea, but they didn't belong here in this room anymore.

He carried the "mementos" box through the house and out the back door. The shed door was slightly open again, and he walked over to close it with his hip as he passed through the yard. As much as he loathed to agree with Marielle about anything, it was starting to get a little wild out here in the back at least.

The gate in the back fence was a little trickier than the shed door, requiring hands Theo didn't really have to spare. He juggled the box, trying to get the latch opened while not dumping everything out on his foot.

"Oh, here." The gate rattled as the young blond man he kept seeing stepped up and opened it from the outside. "You got that okay?"

"Yeah. Thanks," Theo said. He stepped out of his yard and the young man closed the gate behind him.

"Um, why do you have a box of pebbles?"

"That is an excellent question," Theo grumbled. He wasn't really in the mood to chat, but he never liked being outright rude and the people around here were almost aggressively friendly. Besides, this kid seemed like he could use a better influence than that thug he had been speaking with the other day. Theo wondered idly if he had applied to work at the coffee shop. That cheerful barista would be an excellent option for better influence.

"My great-uncle owned this house until he died, and I'm cleaning it out. Slowly. Because the place is stuffed full of weird crap like this. You should have seen the kitchen cupboards. I'm not sure I want to know what he was cooking with the spice shelf full of feathers and seashells."

"Mixed seafood gumbo and fried chicken?" the blond asked. He smiled at Theo, eyes full of laughter.

Theo chuckled. "Somehow I'd be shocked if he knew how to cook at all. He was a bit cracked," Theo said. It didn't feel quite right to him to say that, despite the fact that he didn't know the man. "Well, maybe he was just eccentric. I only met the guy once."

"But you live here now?"

They had reached the bank of the river and Theo crouched, tossing the stones into the water. He picked up one particularly flat one and tried skipping it on the slow, lazy current.

"Hah, three skips! Not bad for being out of practice." Theo grinned up at his companion, who watched the ripples hit the weeds growing at the edges of the bank. There was a sadness about the boy's smile—and how ridiculous was it that Theo was thinking that this young man was a boy. He probably wasn't even a whole decade older than the kid. Adult. Man. God, Theo felt old all of a sudden.

Still, there was something very young and vulnerable about the blond.

"You want a try?" Theo held a stone up and the other man took it, squinting.

"I haven't skipped stones since I was a kid," he said.

"So, what, it's been a whole year?" Theo couldn't help teasing him a bit.

It made the other man roll his eyes and huff at him, but he grinned too. He crouched down, his long, baggy jacket trailing in the dust, and pulled his arm back.

"Take that! Five skips and it almost hit the other side!" the boy crowed.

"Nice!" Theo handed him another one and they skipped them in turns until they ran out of stones. Theo sighed and picked up the sticks from the box, idly tossing them into the water and watching the current move them slowly out of sight. His companion followed suit and together they emptied the box. The last thing, a perfect blue jay feather, Theo simply handed to his new friend.

"My name's Theo. Thanks for the help."

"Quinn," the boy said. He reached out and took the feather carefully in his fingers. "Thanks for letting me hang out with you for a few minutes."

"No problem." Theo peered over at Quinn. He thought about seeing Quinn looking at the Last Pot's help-wanted sign, and talking with the thug. Something was going on here, but it wasn't Theo's place to pry. Still... "If you ever get bored enough to want to haul another box of rocks out here, let me know. It's pretty much all I'm going to be doing these days when I'm not working, and it's going to take a while to get it all out."

Quinn smiled. "I'll keep an eye out for you having more gate trouble."

Theo nodded and turned back to the house. Quinn was gone by the time he stepped through the gate and Theo frowned. It wasn't really like him to worry about a complete stranger, yet here he was, wondering where the boy had gone. With a sigh, he headed back into the house to fetch the books. And figure out what to do with them.

10

MOM CALLS. AGAIN

Theo stepped carefully down the path, listening to the birds chirping in the trees around him. The air smelled fresher than he was used to. Greener, somehow. Why hadn't he been out hiking more often? The trails were right there, behind his house, practically right at his gate. Somewhere nearby water ran, though whether it was a small stream or a wide river he had no idea. It was only the tinkle of the water dancing over a stone or two that he picked up every few steps or so that revealed its presence. He turned his face up in a patch of sun that broke through the branches above and reveled in the simple pleasure of the warmth.

"You should be careful," Ivette's voice murmured in his ear. "Remember, look beneath the surface."

Theo startled and looked around for his neighbor, but there was no one else on the path. He blinked and frowned, wondering if his mind was just churning up bits of old conversations. It had happened to him before, usually when he needed to remember something and it wasn't coming to him. He'd think too hard and then hear someone say something and that would lead him in the direction of the information his brain was hiding from itself.

He was pretty sure he'd never talked to Ivette about the state of reality, though.

He turned and continued down the path, turning the words over in his mind. He peered a little closer at his surroundings, his simple enjoyment marred now by his thoughts. The path curved slightly out of view and something familiar tugged at Theo's memory about the picture it presented. Made him think of coffee and laughter and warmth. The breeze tickled his skin and he felt like the world was teasing him somehow.

The sound of footsteps approaching from the other direction caught his attention and he paused, watching the bend in the path until the steps stopped; whoever it was was standing just hidden by the curve.

"Hello?" Theo called, and it seemed that the whole forest held its breath.

The little noises of the forest died down for a moment at the sound of his voice, then the person stepped forward.

Avery stood there in the path, looking back at him. Well, Theo *thought* it was Avery, at least...

"Avery? What–" It was then that Theo noticed the odd clothes the bouncer wore. The new leather jacket suited him, but it wasn't like any jacket Theo had seen before. It was bright yellow, like a buttercup, and cut longer and more close-fitting than Avery's usual spiked biker-style jacket and had a light gray belt holding it closed at the waist. The leather looked stiffer than he expected for such a cheerful colored garment, as well. The boots resembled the tall biker boots Avery had worn at the bar, but somehow also weren't, though they were still black against the sapphire blue of his pants. He stood on the forest path with the same air of danger he had for those few moments in the bar where he had been the man in charge of security rather than serving drinks. When he had confronted the mugger and driven him off with just a look and an implied threat.

Avery's aqua hair was wild and the air around him glimmered, giving him the illusion of gossamer wings, like if a butterfly's wings had the iridescence of a dragonfly's.

"What's going on?" Theo asked. He wasn't concerned—nothing about this made him afraid—but the simple peace from moments ago had fled. "Avery?"

The forest was abruptly filled with an insistent ringing noise, loud and demanding. Avery turned and disappeared behind the trees. Theo reached out instinctively, flailing with his hand until it came in contact with something.

A table. Theo's fingers brushed the phone that skittered slightly under his touch, still ringing loudly. He groped again and got his hand around it, pulling it to him to swipe at the screen.

"'lo? " he managed to grunt, the sleep clinging to him, trying to drag him back to the forest and the strange almost-Avery. That was the *weirdest* dream.

"Theo, sweetie. You sound like you were asleep."

"Mom, it's..." He pulled his phone back to squint at the display. "It's not quite six a.m. On a Saturday. Yes, I was asleep."

"Oh, I will never get used to these time zones," she grumbled.

Theo sighed and rolled over, blinking at the ceiling. It was a thin excuse and they both knew it.

"What's up, Mom? You don't usually call this early even without the time zones. You're more of a lunch break phone call sort of person. Is something wrong with Dad?"

There was no help for it. He was awake now, dammit. Coffee would soften this blow.

"Oh, no. Your dad's fine. I'm fine. We're all just fine, hon."

Theo blinked, pausing on the stairs. "Um, Mom?"

She sighed. "I just miss you, sweetie. I woke up thinking it would be a wonderful day to meet you for lunch and discuss the new findings in the archaeology world, and then I remembered that you're all the way across the country. I still don't understand why you had to move so far away out there."

"Because Penny threw me out when I broke up with her and I had nowhere to live. You know that you and Dad don't have the room anymore since you moved, either. Besides, this is a nice house." Theo tripped over the box of twigs and pebbles he had cleared out of his room yesterday. "Well, it will be when I get it cleaned up anyway. And the people are surprisingly friendly. I like it here."

"But it's not your home, Theo. What was wrong with that sweet little apartment you lived in?"

It had Penny in it? Theo didn't actually say it out loud. Even uncaffeinated he was smarter than that.

"It wasn't home to me, Mom, and there were too many tainted memories." They'd had this discussion several times. For some reason, his parents *really* didn't like Gruncle Garfield. "And I literally just pointed out that Penny threw me out of it."

"You could have found someplace until this thing with Penny sorts itself out," his mom tried again.

"Sorts itself... Mom, she cheated on me. With the man that claimed to be my best friend and business partner. Remember that part? Then she blamed *me* for it because I wasn't willing to fund her early retirement lifestyle with my

inheritance? *And then* she said it was fine since I was probably sleeping around anyway because that's what bisexual
men do? Remember that part?" Theo wished the coffee
pot would finish faster, then gave up and swapped the pot
out for a mug until it was full. "She showed me what her
true colors were in the end, Mom, and they weren't pretty.
And you keep going back and forth, telling me that she was
never any good for me, then trying to get us back together
the next time we talk. You need to pick one opinion,
Mom."

"But all those years, sweetie."

"Years of living with her false face. Years of thinking
my life was one thing but it was really another. Years of
living..." Theo flashed back to his dream. "Years of living
in a world that wasn't at all what it seemed."

"Theo?"

"She just wanted someone to fund her lifestyle, Mom.
Sure she had a job—part-time at the end of our relationship
if you'll recall—but mostly what she did was go out to lunch
and shop with her friends. And, you know, sleep around
with my business partner and not-so-best friend." Theo
sighed, taking a long gulp of his coffee. "What is this really
about, Mom? Because I know you don't want me to be
miserable, tied to a cheater."

"I just want you to come home, I guess," his mom said
quietly. "They're friendly there, you said? Your neighbors?
That's good at least. You need a few good friends, and if
you're going to cut everyone off from here..."

"I only cut off my ex and the jerk who slept with her,
and the people that were very clearly *not* my friends. I still
chat with people online and I talk to you on the phone
more than I ever did before I moved."

"I suppose that's true. I just..." She sighed again and
Theo felt bad about being so annoyed. She wasn't really

trying to control his life. Not any more than usual, anyhow. She hadn't liked the idea of him moving so far away, and she seemed to think that just living in Gruncle Garfield's house would somehow change Theo.

Maybe she was right. He did feel different. Not that he was going to tell his mother that. The Avery from his dream floated into his mind's eye and it was tangled up with the image of Avery standing there, facing off with the mugger. Somehow Theo could clearly see the bright yellow jerkin against the dirty brick wall and the shimmering, wild aura surrounding Avery in the alley. It felt like he was right on the edge of something but was missing some bit of information he needed to make sense of everything.

Theo shook his head sharply to clear the crazy thoughts so he could answer his mother.

"Mom, I wasn't exactly the world's most social butterfly back in Omaha, and now I'm just the same Theo but further away. If it will make you feel better we can set up video chats once a week or something. You can see my face. How's that? And I'm making some nice friends here. A family a few blocks over with some really great kids, and the guy I met at the bar has gotten to be a really good friend. I don't miss the people who gave me dirty looks and glares when I left a cheater, as if it was *my* fault."

He talked with her for a few more minutes and hung up the phone. When he finished his coffee he got up and poured more into his cup and stared blearily out at his backyard. Jorge had offered his older boy to come to mow for him today as they ate brownies to avoid the irritating detective. He liked the idea of a neighborhood kid doing the work, instead of the faceless landscaping corporation that had been handling it.

Maybe he should plant a garden? That cat was out there, sitting near the shed, carefully tidying up its paws. It stopped to glance up at Theo, staring at him as if repri-manding him for slacking off. Theo felt a smile starting to form as the creature seemed to sigh before finishing up and then standing with a luxurious stretch and sauntering off. It stopped at the door to the shed to nose at it. Then with a pointed glance back at Theo, the cat leaped over the gate and disappeared from view.

Huh. Theo had the strangest feeling that the cat was trying to tell him something. That was completely ridicu-lous of course, but maybe there was something in the shed?

Theo started to go out and investigate but the cool morning breeze on his bare skin stopped him with the real-ization that he was still in his boxers and nothing else. While yes, it was his yard and he could go nude if he pleased, the thought of Ivette glancing over from her kitchen window, immaculately dressed in her signature twinset and pearls...

Theo shuddered and jogged upstairs to throw on some clothes. When he eventually got out to the shed, there was no sign that anyone had ever been in his yard. The shed was as empty as it had been the last time Theo peeked into it Still immaculately tidy, everything in its place. There was a small smudge of dried mud by the door, but other-wise nothing obvious. Theo frowned and scratched his fingers through his beard.

Maybe he should get a lock for the door? That seemed like the simplest solution. He tugged the tarp off the lawn-mower to check that there was gas for it and was somewhat surprised to find it was an old-fashioned push mower. A fancy, expensive-looking one, but still. He tugged it into the middle of the shed, testing how easily it moved and how well the blades turned, and all the things he could think of, which honestly wasn't much.

Well, hopefully Artie wouldn't have any trouble with it. The boy was twelve, he thought Jorge had said? And if the kid did have trouble, Theo would thank him anyway and still pay him for his time. Maybe he'd have the kid help him haul the sticks to the river instead.

Theo stepped back into the sunshine of his yard and closed the shed door behind him. Whatever else this morning held in store for him could wait. It was too damn early and he needed more coffee to deal with it. More coffee and maybe a few minutes figuring out the sleep mode on his phone so his mom couldn't wake him up again.

11

BREAKFAST WITH QUINN

B eing woken at way-too-early o'clock by his mother was not doing Theo any favors. He trudged into the Last Pot and blinked at the menu board.

"Oh, wow. This is the groggiest we've ever seen you," the friendly barista—whose name turned out to be Alair, which Theo learned on his second visit—said with a grin. "Not that we've seen you a lot in a week, but still."

"My mother called this morning, well before civilized creatures are out of bed. Because she *misses* me." Theo blinked at Alair and sighed.   "I was doing okay until I sat down for a few minutes to sort through some old books I found in the back of the pantry. That old man stuck stuff in all sorts of crazy places."

Alair cocked his head. "What was he doing reading in the pantry? Were they cookbooks?"

"History, from what I could tell. One was in German."

"Oof." Alair grinned and put Theo's order in quickly and the grumpy barista—Alice—sent him a nod and almost even smiled her greeting which made him grin.

"Hey, are you in trouble or something?   A detective

came in asking about you and some other folks from your neighborhood. Our boss took him into the office for about half an hour, and wouldn't let the guy talk to us cause we were kind of slammed, but..." Alair scrunched up his face.

Theo groaned. "One of the HOA president's minions decided that I know all about the vandalism since I moved here around the time it started. Because, you know, I moved over a thousand miles just to deface some private property. For fun."

Alair rolled his eyes and laughed. "Everyone needs a hobby, I guess!"

"Well, as irritating as he may be I have nothing to hide. If he asks again I don't mind if you tell him how I like my coffee."

"I'll let him know you like it as bitter as your soul," Alice called. "But with a touch of whole milk foam to lighten your day."

That made Theo laugh. "Thanks, Alice! If you can't trust your barista or your bartender, you're in sorry shape indeed."

Alair laughed and even Alice sent him a cheerful smirk.

As he stepped aside to seek out a table, he realized that the cafe was fairly busy for so early on a Saturday. He found a small table near the kitchen door and sat, letting the sounds of the coffee machine and the general rumble of other people's conversations wash over him.

"Oh, good morning," a voice intruded and he blinked his eyes open. When had he closed them?

"Oh, Quinn. Morning. Here for breakfast?"

The young man looked less rumpled than before, but only just. His hair was slightly tamed, and his clothes were mostly clean, with his T-shirt tucked into his jeans under his baggy jacket.

"No, actually. I was interviewing. I need a job."

Quinn shrugged and grimaced ruefully. "It's tough to find one since I didn't finish high school. Is what it is, you know?"

"People get too hung up on bits of paper, I think," Theo said, mostly because he didn't know what else to say.

Quinn's stomach rumbled loud enough to make Theo raise his eyebrows. Quinn's shoulders curled in a bit, but he kept his chin up.

"Join me? For breakfast?" Theo wasn't sure where the invitation had come from but he found he meant it.

"Oh, I can't–"

"My treat, in hopeful celebration of your incipient employment." Theo smiled, making Quinn chuckle.

"You're going to be pushy, aren't you?" Quinn asked, but he didn't sound upset. More like relieved.

"Like you wouldn't believe. Go order something and tell Alair you're with me." Theo glanced past Quinn to Alair who was keeping an eye on them while he tidied up after the customers who had just left. Theo darted his eyes to Quinn and quirked an eyebrow, and Alair winked and nodded.

Quinn returned soon with a mug of plain black coffee and a little number placard for some food. He put the stand down at the edge of the table where Alair or the other barista whose name Theo hadn't caught yet could see it easily, and almost sighed into the chair.

"The coffee here's wonderful, isn't it?" Theo asked after Quinn had a sip.

"It's good. I haven't had real coffee for a while." Quinn took another sip, savoring it. "I usually try to save my money for the laundromat, you know? As much as I would love better coffee, clean clothes sort of trumps that in the budget. If I get hired, though, I get a meal here on days I work more than four hours and free drip coffee. As long as I don't clean out several pots a day, she said." Quinn grinned and Theo chuckled as he was expected to.

There was something bright about this kid—and yes, he was aware that Quinn was at least old enough to get a job on his own, which meant he was an adult. But Quinn somehow exuded *youth* and Theo couldn't help responding to that.

"I'll keep my fingers crossed for you, then. Wouldn't want to deprive a man of his coffee, after all," Theo said.

The conversation stalled when Alair brought over two trays of food and slid them onto the table, whisking the numbers away when he left. They both fell to eating, Quinn again savoring each bite of food. Theo was full of questions, and none of them felt especially polite, but...

"Do you need help, Quinn? I mean, I could put in a reference for you or something." Theo stumbled over his words. He didn't usually put himself out for other people, but maybe it was the smaller town sort of feeling that this neighborhood had, or the vulnerability that Quinn tried to hide. There was something about him that made Theo feel protective of the young man as if he were Quinn's older brother or something.

Quinn smiled and shook his head. "Thanks, though. I mean, you bought me breakfast, that's already a lot. Thank you."

Theo shrugged. "I was awake at stupid o'clock this morning and needed something to shake me out of my funk. I should thank you."

"Something woke you up early?" Quinn looked spooked as he asked.

Theo decided not to ask about the strange reaction and just sighed. "My mother called. Before six. Because she wants me to move back to Omaha even though I have no place to live there and like hell I'm moving back in with them to sleep on my parents' sofa or wherever she thinks I'll stay. That's why I'm even awake at eight o'clock on a Saturday, let alone out and about."

Quinn's expression was impossible to ignore this time. Resignation and heartbreak. "Must be nice, though. To have a mom that wants you around like that."

Ouch. Right in the guilt.

"Your mom less than maternal?" Theo guessed.

"Dead, actually. I can't even remember her. My dad though, yeah." Quinn sighed. "That's why I need this job so badly."

Theo didn't know what to say to that so he stayed quiet, finishing off his eggs and toast. As much as he loved the fancy sandwiches they had here, for breakfast he was a fairly simple guy. After a long minute, Quinn started talking again.

"Mom died when I was not quite a year old. I guess she was sick a lot anyway, then the stress of having a baby was too much," Quinn pushed the last bite of potato around his plate and didn't look up at Theo. "I have a few photos of her in my bag, holding me as a baby, and she looked so happy. Dad did too back then. Proud, you know? I don't remember him ever looking like that in real life. Just in those pictures."

Theo put his fork down and picked up his mug. Quinn wasn't looking at him anymore, but Theo kept his attention on the young man.

"I don't remember my dad ever being particularly happy with me around. I think I reminded him too much of my mom, mostly, but I was also not the son he wanted."

Theo must have made a noise because Quinn looked up with a wry smile.

"I am fully aware of how common that story is, but I

don't think it's going to end exactly the way you think. Close, though, probably." Quinn swallowed the last of his coffee. "Dad wanted a football star. At least, someone he could play ball with in the park or whatever. Basketball would have been okay too. Me? I was a swimmer and I ran track in high school for a year, which was at least acceptable, but I was never the beefy tough kid he wanted. No, I was the weird kid who loved school and enjoyed studying."

"Nothing wrong with that," Theo said.

Quinn shrugged. "I guess. I tried. I went out for the football team and came back with a rotator cuff injury. I couldn't even swim for a while after that. Making the football team was out of the question, and the coach was really nice about it, worried about my shoulder, you know? But for Dad it was the last straw. He started telling me about how much of a disappointment I was, and why did he keep wasting money taking care of me when all I ever did was hide away in my room with a 'damn worthless book.' His words. He just hates intellectuals or something. I still don't understand it."

"Wow. You're right, that's a twist I wasn't expecting." Theo frowned. "Why would he get so upset with you for not making the team? You got injured."

"I don't know. He always hated that I read so much. He kept enrolling me in sports clubs and stuff when I was a kid. It was an obsession with him. Baseball, soccer, ice hockey one year when I was in elementary school, and that was a horrible few months. I liked the skating though, that was fun." Quinn's quicksilver smile turned into a frown. "I can't even tell you the number of different martial arts classes he made me take. I swear there was a new one every year, and when I didn't take to one he'd just stick me in another."

"Was he a fighter?"

"Nah, just happy to pitch in with a punch or three if someone needed help. I have no idea why he was so determined that I learn to fight. I kind of enjoyed some of the classes, though. The more philosophical ones and stuff. I picked up a little bit of Japanese and Chinese too. The languages, I mean. And a few words of Korean." Quinn grinned briefly.

"But after that last argument, I couldn't stay there. I packed a bag and left when he polished off the case of beer from the garage and passed out in front of the TV. That was a few months ago now." Quinn grimaced. "I really wasn't thinking, honestly. But..."

His shoulders slumped and his story petered out. Theo wasn't sure what to say to that. His folks had frowned on some of his interests and his mother had absolutely encouraged him to take a certain path and not another, but it had been nothing like this. If he had not been at all interested in science or writing about it, he was fairly sure that they would have supported him in that choice. Artist or plumber or whatever he had wanted to do, as long as he had been happy and practical about it.

"So, where are you staying now?"

A slight shiver ran through Quinn's hands, and if Theo hadn't been looking he might have missed it.

"I'm staying with a friend," Quinn said. "Well, with a guy I know. He was pissed when he heard what happened with my dad. He went through something similar with his own family, though he didn't run away, he was kicked out. He's sort of starting to scare me a bit though, so I really hope I get this job so I can save up for an apartment or something."

It was Theo's turn to frown. Some long-ignored instinct was stirring and he had a bad feeling, reminding him briefly of Ivette and her comment about trusting her gut. It was like a sour tingle in his stomach, warning him that something was important and not in a good way. He couldn't ignore it. "Scaring you?"

Quinn shrugged. "He..." Quinn stopped and glanced up at Theo and paled. Then he coughed and moved to look around the cafe as he talked. Subtle this kid was not. "He's always been mad at his family for kicking him out, but he found something about a month ago that made him a lot worse. He's been drinking more and I dunno... He's gotten angrier."

Theo didn't like the way the hair on his arms and the back of his neck started to stand up, and he shivered a bit, rubbing at his forearm for a moment hoping to drive the feeling away.

"Are you in danger?" Theo asked.

Quinn pressed his lips together tightly and brought his attention back to the tabletop. "I don't think so," he said slowly. "I think that if I can talk him down a bit, he'll be okay, but he doesn't always listen to me. I'm afraid that he's going to get into stuff that's bigger than he can handle, you know? He.... he wasn't always this intense about his family. He was angry, but that's pretty understandable. But now it's like he's obsessed about it all, and..."

Theo let Quinn pick his words.

"He wasn't what his family wanted him to be either," Quinn said. "He'll be okay. Yeah, there's a problem with expectations of kids and so on–"

"Which has been the theme of today's conversation," Theo said with a smirk. "My mom was very insistent on what she thought should be my choice of future, but I actually like archaeology and random science reporting, so it's not much of a burden. And as irritating as she can be, I know she loves me."

"Woah, is that what you do? That's so cool!" Quinn's eyes lit up and he leaned forward. "What sort of archaeology?"

Theo laughed at the sudden eagerness and told his young friend about the latest article he was writing.

12

SATURDAY CHORES

A rtie Cardoso was stronger than he looked.

He came over with his friend Holly, a bubbly, strawberry blonde girl who immediately shook her head at the state of Theo's yard and started in on weeding. Artie went right for the push-mower, though, and had no trouble at all with the heavy machine when even Theo had had a bit of a struggle to push the thing onto the grass. The kids even trimmed the hedge in front so it was a bit tidier. Artie said that it would be good for the plants, in the long run, to be cared for, and the twelve-year-old made the pronouncement with such matter-of-fact bluntness that Theo just nodded and let him do as he pleased. He certainly couldn't deny that the yard looked lusher and more alive in the boy's wake.

Both kids were firm about what the yard needed, and hiring them for the whole summer was the first step. Theo bit back a grin at the somber faces as the pair made their business deal, finalizing it with a solemn handshake each.

Artie also mentioned that he had found the box of camping gear tucked into the back corner of the shed when he put the mower away, and Theo suddenly connected it to Quinn. If Quinn was sleeping in his shed to get away from the older, apparently angrier, young man then Theo would leave it alone for now. He didn't mind, though it wasn't a situation that could last too long.

Artie and Holly were sent on their way after being handed some cash and one of Stacy's brownies each. They skipped off with a promise to return the following week to do it all over again. Theo was glad to know the pair was on the job, and the whole yard felt more alive, even though they simply left the grass freshly mowed and the hedge tamed into tidiness.

He stood on his porch and glanced across the street and down a few houses at the new "perfect" house that had been stuck between older places. Most of the houses on his street had remained untouched, thank goodness, with older, established residents living in them.

As he turned back to his door he noticed a dark sedan parked down the street that looked remarkably like the one that had been in front of the Wolf the afternoon before, and Theo wondered if it was the misguided detective still haring off after Candace's "tip."

"Those two will be good for your yard. You keep them coming back, Theo. That boy may be just coming into his power, but he'll have the place put back to rights soon enough, and Holly's no slouch, either."

Theo turned and greeted his neighbor with a nod. She was wearing dark jeans today, and her cardigan and the shell underneath were a soft mauve, but the pearls were still in place as she sat on her rocker.

"I'm not sure it was particularly out of sorts, but I was thinking of maybe some flower beds in the back. If he's willing to help with that I'd have to get more baked goods though," Theo answered.

Ivette laughed, her eyes crinkling at the corners. "That is true enough. At his age, he'll work for food. Teenagers so often can't get enough as they grow like weeds. Those Cardoso boys especially. But being in the sunshine and the dirt is just as good for him as a fourth meal in the day."

Theo nodded. He remembered when he was a teen and his mother had despaired of him ever not wandering around with a snack in hand. Wait, his brain caught up with something and he had to ask, "Power? What do you mean by 'his power'?" That was a weird way to put "growing teenager-ness."

"A garden is a lovely idea," Ivette said, cheerfully ignoring his question. "Angelica, sage, rosemary. Make sure you plant those in there along the river. Wouldn't hurt to do along the front, too, to keep unwanted visitors away. I saw the detective paid you a visit the other day. He's been back a few times, poking around, I've noticed."

Theo chuckled through his frown. "Marielle and her cronies have decided that since I didn't fall in with their preferences, I *must* be the guy who's painting all those tags all over town. So she sicced one of her buddies and the detective on me and made a big scene at the bar at lunchtime. I guess he thought if he ditched Candace I'd be less annoyed by the whole thing and talk to him. He keeps catching me when I'm out, and I keep telling him I don't know anything and please go away."

"You certainly didn't give him much chance, did you?" She twinkled.

"I'm not a fan of bullies." Theo shrugged.

Ivette just nodded.

"Listen, do you know where I could maybe get rid of some of my great-uncle's books and stuff? The house is crammed full and I'm finally making some headway, but I don't know anywhere to take the stuff I'm not keeping."

Ivette sipped at her drink and considered him. "You might want to keep more than you think you do," she said finally. "But yes. If you go out as if you are heading to the Three-Legged Wolf, then go past it, there is a secondhand shop. You can take some things there. Baz knows what could be dangerous and what is safe enough, and who to sell such things to."

"Fantastic. Thanks," Theo said after a moment of blinking at yet another strange statement. Ivette was on a roll again today. "And I don't know what all is in there yet, really. I just finished clearing out the room I'm staying in, and it was mostly magpie stuff. Twigs and pebbles and shiny coins, you know?"

She grinned again and nodded. "I do. Your uncle, he *was* a bit of a magpie." Ivette giggled. "Not literally, of course, but there was certainly an affinity."

"Yeah." Theo chuckled. "Anyhow, I'd better get some lunch and keep on cleaning. Seems a good day for it. Maybe start on one of the more stuffed-full rooms."

"Indeed," she answered with a nod. "Oh, if you were planning to drive anywhere, it's also the day to put it off. There was another rash of tagging last night and traffic is a disaster on the main roads."

"Seriously? Well, good thing I wasn't planning anything in particular, then."

Ivette nodded again and sipped her drink. Theo smiled and nodded his farewell and headed back inside.

I t was a few hours later and he had a full box of stuff to take down to the riverbank. He had poked around, giving the dining room and kitchen greater scrutiny, and found feathers from a dozen different birds in with the table linens (which were badly in need of a wash and some air) and more pebbles in the spice cupboard—which smelled faintly of cinnamon and pine forest—and coins everywhere. Coins from all over the world and, Theo suspected, from places that no longer existed, erased from maps thanks to politics and war and general human nonsense. The coins he put in a pretty bowl he found and put it on the dining room breakfront, similar to the bowl he still had upstairs in his room.

It was late enough that he felt he'd earned a break and taking the box down to the river and then having a walk in the late-afternoon sunshine seemed like a wonderful plan. Then maybe he would brave the bar for an evening, just for a change of scenery. He didn't have any projects due for a bit and honestly, hiding in his house from all the socializing hadn't helped much. He didn't feel particularly social, but continuing to rattle around the empty house made him a bit anxious tonight.

Theo was well aware of how weird it was to go someplace crowded to avoid social interactions, but he had found over the years that places like bars or restaurants made it easy for him to people watch and enjoy the general energy of human contact without actually having to talk to anyone beyond giving his order. There were signals that people usually respected for a lone man in a public place, and he knew perfectly well how to play that game.

It had made Penny crazy when she wanted to go out and be the center of attention, and Theo had made it clear from his body language that visitors were not welcome at their table. Honestly, the more he thought about their relationship, the more he realized that he should have gotten away from her sooner. Hindsight and all that, he guessed.

As he closed the gate which squeaked in complaint

behind him, he saw the bright shine of spray paint flash in the sunshine.

"Son of a—" Theo put the box down and cursed loudly. He peered closer at the tag on his fence, half on his gate. It was some unreadable symbol, no doubt the tagger's name or some message written in such a stylized way as to render it illegible. Further obscuring it was what seemed to be soot as if something had burned hard up against the fence somehow without damaging it. It looked like the paint might come off easily enough with some paint thinner and a little elbow grease. Still, something about the thing made Theo shiver as goosebumps raced up his arms.

"Well, hell. Guess I'll be painting the damn fence," Theo grumbled.

He kept his grumbles up all the way to the edge of the river where he squatted and put the box down. He set the box at his feet then picked up one edge, tipping the whole thing on its side so the contents could rattle and slide into a heap on the muddy ground. Once he upended the whole thing and moved the box, he frowned at the pile and muttered to himself uncharitable thoughts on the subject of packrats.

Now it looked like someone had dumped a box of twigs and pebbles out here. Granted, that's what happened, but littering was still littering, so he started picking the twigs and sticks out and tossing them into the flowing water and let his mind wander. He wondered if Quinn had gotten that job at the Last Pot, and what his mom was doing right now, and if he actually should take the speaking engagement his agent was trying to land for him. After a bit he just watched the sticks float away from him, tracing the slow current of the shallow river.

"Well, that looks soothing as hell," Avery said from behind him, making Theo jump. His position didn't exactly lend itself to stability so of course he started to tip toward the water, and he braced for his inevitable soaking.

"Whoa! Gotcha!" Avery's warm hands caught his shoulders and tugged him back to safety. "Sorry for startling you, I thought you heard me walk up.

Theo sat back on his butt, a little dusty but that was better than being soggy from falling in the stupid river. "Hey. No harm done, I guess."

"What're you up to there?" Avery glanced at the box of debris with stark curiosity.

"Gruncle Garfield was a damn magpie. I thought that when I first moved here and I still think it's the best word for it. That house is crammed with what any six-year-old would call 'treasures,' you know?" He nodded at the box. "Sticks and feathers and interesting stones and shiny coins and bits of broken jewelry and what have you. This is all just from the kitchen and the dining room. I haven't even started on the rest of the house, outside the room I'm sleeping in. And don't even get me started on the books. They're literally everywhere."

Avery offered him a hand and he took it, letting the other man pull him to his feet.

"I figured I'd dump this stuff outside here where it belongs, then sort out the books and the coins and everything else later. My neighbor Ivette told me there's a secondhand shop nearby." Theo brushed himself off. "Hey, there's another question. Know where to get paint around here? I've got some covering up to do."

"Covering up?" Avery frowned and ran his gaze up and down Theo.

"Uh…" Theo hoped his beard would hide the blush he felt starting. "Yeah. The vandal hit my fence."

"Oh." Avery's expression darkened and he turned to look at Theo's house. Only about half the tag was visible from here. "That's not good. Really not good. I heard they tagged Marielle's house the other day too. And a few of her closest buddies' places."

"That's no excuse for trying to get someone arrested," Theo grumbled.

"I agree. In hindsight, I don't think that cop was entirely on her side of things, but yeah. I don't like that woman–I never have, to be entirely honest with you–but the other day seemed an extra layer of pissy. And now you've been tagged, too? You gonna call him and report it?"

"Maybe." Theo grimaced, not loving the idea of calling the detective that seemed to be following him around, and actually inviting him over on purpose.

Avery shook his head and seemed to be turning something over in his mind. Theo took the opportunity to kick his foot over the rest of his pile of debris, nudging the pebbles and feathers and whatnot around a bit with his toe so they weren't just piled up in a lump anymore.

"So hey. I'm glad I ran into you. I'm heading into work soon and was stopping by on my way. I planned to go 'round to the front door but here you are," Avery said. He turned back to Theo and stuck his hands into the pockets of his leather jacket. It was hip-length and a soft-looking black with shiny silver buckles like you expect from a not-quite-punk style leather jacket. Nothing stiff or oddly armor-like about it at all. Definitely not yellow.

Though his scarf underneath was.

"Yeah?" Theo was not feeling terribly witty.

"Yeah. I, uh." Avery paused and Theo had to blink for a moment as he watched the top of Avery's ears turn pink. "This is stupid. Here. I wish I had thought of it sooner, but it wasn't until Wednesday night that I did, then I couldn't catch Fitz at home until late Thursday night, then he needed a little time to make it."

Avery yanked his hand out of his pocket and thrust it out to Theo, who automatically put his hand up to receive whatever was still hidden in Avery's fingers. A small thing dropped into his hand and he peered at it.

It was an intriguing little pendant, like a bag a bit bigger than a quarter, but made of a soft metal mesh with some sort of fabric inside that Theo could just see hints of when the mesh flexed. It shone almost like it was reflecting more than just the afternoon sunlight, and whatever the small bag contained was heavier than he expected. The chain flowed around his fingers to drape prettily in a swinging loop. The whole thing somehow looked both delicate and sturdy at the same time.

"What's this?" Theo asked.

"It's a protection charm. A friend of mine–Fitz–makes them and he's damn good. But with the mugging the other day, Marielle on the warpath, and that detective listening to any part of her ranting, and now with the vandal so close, apparently, and..." Avery shrugged and stared pointedly out at the river flowing past them. "I mean, you don't have to wear it, but I just get a bit protective, you know? I like knowing my friends are safe even if I'm not around. It's a thing with me."

Theo blinked at Avery, whose ears were definitely pink now. It was amusing and contrasted with the aqua hair and tough adult-punk look he had going on. Then the words really penetrated.

"Your friends?"

Avery just shrugged again, carefully not meeting Theo's eyes. "I mean yeah. You seem pretty cool, and you defended the Cardoso boys, and you stand up to Marielle and her crew. We need more folk like you around here."

Theo eyed the man. At the bar he had seemed friendly and confident, then when he put his metaphorical security hat on he seemed intimidating and confident. Now, he seemed to be shy. It was kind of adorable.

Theo started to say something but glanced down at the bag. A protection charm, huh? Magic was absolute rubbish, of course, but the gesture was very sweet and it certainly wouldn't actually hurt anything.

"There's nothing illegal in here, is there?" Theo exaggerated a squint and Avery laughed.

"Nah. Fitz wouldn't do that to his customers."

Theo cocked an eyebrow at the other man for a long moment, just to watch Avery get flustered again, then he dropped the loop of chain over his head. The bag settled over his sternum, warmer than Theo expected it to be, and a comforting weight against his chest. A shiver rippled over him, and he did feel strangely safer. Probably because no matter what he told himself, it was really good to know he had someone that cared nearby.

"Thanks," he said.

"No problem." Avery grinned.

13

PORCH COFFEE

After giving Theo the "magic protection charm"–Theo mentally rolled his eyes every time he thought that–Avery gave Theo a more practical gift: a promise to come by in the morning and help clear out some of the books in the back room with the suggestion that Avery's cousin might like some of them. So this morning Theo carefully made extra coffee and sat on the front porch with a steaming mug full and wrapped up in a thick blanket against the February cold, just enjoying the morning and ignoring the weight of the small charm bag against his chest.

Even if it was strangely comforting and he had made a point to put it back on after his shower.

He definitely wasn't going to think about why he had slept with the thing.

He still didn't have any new projects, and if nothing picked up soon he was going to get a bit worried. He had been here in Whitelake for a little over a month, and while he had enough to live on thanks to Gruncle Garfield and the sale of his half of the business, inactivity wasn't his style. His mom had called again last night, and after his long day he wasn't really in the mood to be guilt-tripped into moving back and he had snapped at her.

So now he felt bad about that too. He didn't want to hurt his mom's feelings but she had to let go. He was well into adulthood and didn't want to be smothered by his mother just because *she* was having a hard time with *his* breakup.

"You look terrible," Avery said as he turned up the walk. "Did you sleep at all?"

Theo growled in answer, then waved at the insulated coffeepot he'd brought out with him. "Mugs are in the kitchen though, and milk and all that, if you take it."

"Thanks." Avery disappeared inside and Theo kept staring at the street, watching the occasional jogger but mostly just enjoying the peace. This corner of the neighborhood seemed to be blessedly quiet. He wasn't sure he could have stood living nearer to the entrance of the subdivision, over near Marielle and the mostly newer homes. Here along the river were largely the older houses, thank goodness, and the older residents.

It was more like a small town than any suburban street. Not like the suburbs he was used to, and like Marielle and her cronies probably wanted to create: a tidy, uniform area where people barely acknowledged each other. The sort of easy friendship and neighborly chats that Theo had experienced in the past few weeks were likely anathema to the HOA board.

Now that Marielle had forced an acquaintance and Ivette had allowed him a brief audience, all his neighbors had introduced themselves one way or another. He now knew not only Ivette and Avery and the Cardosos, but others as well. The elderly man down the street had stopped while walking his dog to pass a few minutes of small talk, and the sisters who lived on the corner had come by and brought a cheerful bouquet of pale pink roses and delicate hydrangea to welcome him to the neighborhood.

Everyone who came to introduce themselves brought some small welcoming gift or offer of a friendly service of some sort–help raking leaves in the fall or produce from their garden when it was time to harvest, or business cards if he ever needed plumbers or electricians or in one amusing case, a jeweler. All the services came with the "neighborhood discount" promise, which left Theo feeling flattered but slightly off-balance. He did begin to understand how Garfield had ended up with such a full house, though, when a child solemnly handed him a sticky pinecone and told him it was "Cause welcome."

It was... nice.

The pinecone was now sitting next to his laptop on the diningroom table, and Theo felt not at all ashamed of it.

"Hey, sorry it took so long," Avery said when he stepped back out and reached for the pot. "It's been a bit since I've been in there so I got a little lost."

Theo grunted in response and they both settled on the porch to watch the world go by for a bit longer. After a while, Theo felt compelled to speak, even though the silence was surprisingly easy between them.

"Sorry. I'm just exhausted this morning for some reason. Didn't sleep well, I guess."

Avery nodded in sympathy. "I get that. Some nights I get back from the bar so wound up that even if I sleep in till noon I'm still wiped out."

Theo nodded and drank the rest of his coffee. The small charm felt warm against his chest, tucked under his shirt.

"Did you hear that there was another mugging last

night? Right here in the neighborhood," Avery asked after he took another sip.

Theo frowned and looked over at him. The morning sun made the blue in Avery's hair sparkle like the sea in the Caribbean and he had just a second where he would have sworn there were iridescent wings tucked in behind Avery. He shook his head to clear the fanciful thoughts and Avery took that as his response.

"Apparently one of the New Crew was getting out of her car and some kid in a hoodie and a ski mask came up and waved a knife at her. Took her purse and her engagement ring." Avery pursed his lips. "That detective guy showed up at the bar asking if anyone in the line to get in had seen anything. Actually drove some customers off from the line. Jackass had to know that would happen if he showed up and flashed his badge around, and he did it anyway. Glad I was on the door, though. I told him that if he wanted to come inside he'd either have to show me his warrant or get in the back of the line like any other customer."

Theo snorted. He'd have liked to have seen that. "Bet that rumpled his expensive blazer."

Avery grinned now. "Sure did. I guess he doesn't hear the word *no* often enough." The grin dropped away for a moment. "He asked about you again too."

"God. I really am going to have to call a lawyer, aren't I?" Theo groaned. "I swear the guy's been following me. I keep seeing him when I go out to get groceries or whatever, and he's called me twice, and approached me three times. I guess he's just doing his job, but man. He just rubs me the wrong way. He's all smarmy good-cop, like he's waiting for me to slip up or something."

"I agree. He's too curious about the neighborhood. Might not be a bad idea to let your lawyer know. Just in case." Avery nodded. "And he seems to have connected the muggings to the vandalism, which I'd think would let you off the hook, at least. I don't like that he's pestering you. Anyway. I told him that if he wants to hear bar gossip then he still needed to wait in line and pay the cover. Or go listen to Marielle and her rich bitch HOA people."

"Well, thanks for that." Theo sat back on the bench and watched as the cat slunk up the sidewalk, stopping every so often to sniff at something he couldn't see. It ducked under one of the bushes that lined his front walk and popped out of the shadows underneath onto the sunshine-drenched lawn.

"Good morning, kitty," Theo said. He had a long-standing rule that it was only smart to be polite to strange animals, and this one seemed more like a neighbor than a stranger at this point, keeping an eye on him and his house and making sure Theo knew it. Besides, the cat was probably keeping the rodent population in check all on its own.

The cat meowed, then stuck out its front paws in a stretch that rippled all the way through the tip of its tail before hopping lightly up onto the porch and joining them.

"You have a cat?" Avery asked. He held his fingers out in greeting and the cat deigned to sniff at them before bumping its head against Avery's knuckles. He chuckled and ran his fingers over the cat's head and down its dark fur.

"More accurate to say the cat has me. It started coming by a while ago. Maybe a couple of weeks? I was on the back deck trying to avoid my writing and it just sauntered up and hopped onto the table and lay down in the patch of sun next to my laptop. Stayed all afternoon." Theo reached out to give the cat some attention as well, and the engine rumble of purring rose around them. "Oh, you just like the attention, huh?"

The cat murred and settled down between them, allowing them to keep petting while it closed its eyes.

"You're right. I think you've been adopted." Avery smirked. "It's funny. I don't see a lot of cats around here. Sometimes in the woods across the river, but not often in the neighborhood. Too many dogs and what have you, I think."

"What have you?" Theo laughed. "You mean the attack squirrels?"

Avery glanced up at him but didn't elaborate.

"Cats are surprising creatures. They sense things that even other animals can't. They..." Avery's brow wrinkled as he looked for the right words. "They know things, and they're warriors in their own way. Protectors when they choose to care about something. There's a reason they're eagerly sought by witches for familiars." He shook his head. "I'd say that if you've been adopted while living in this neighborhood, you're in better shape than you think, Marielle's smear campaign or not."

"That's a very interesting way to look at it," Theo said.

"Well, I call 'em as I see 'em," Avery said.

"So back to the subject, who got mugged? And what is a New Crew?" Theo asked.

Avery huffed a half chuckle and rolled his eyes. "The New Crew is what a lot of us call the more recent residents. The ones who live in the cookie-cutter boxes the developer put up? We, uh… We had a different name for them, but then one of the kids heard it and, well." He grinned again now. "We had to come up with something else."

Theo raised an eyebrow at Avery but didn't comment.

"So one of Marielle's people got mugged, you said? Near here?"

"Apparently." Avery frowned. "Between the vandalism, the traffic, and the muggings lately, *something* is going on. I wasn't too worried until it all started settling in right around here. I mean, I used to live in a much busier area than this–I grew up near Washington, DC, and traffic was never less than terrible, and some of the tags there were actually kind of comforting landmarks. But here…"

Theo nodded. Some aspects of city life were just so *normal*. "It does feel out of place here, you're right. Big city situations plaguing a town that for all its population and the college and all, is really still a small town despite the New Crew's best efforts."

"Exactly." Avery nodded. The cat yawned and stretched and tucked its head down onto its paws, rolling over a bit onto Theo's leg in the process. "Oh, guess you can give him a name then."

"Yeah. This is the closest I've been to him yet and I didn't want to presume." Theo rested his hand on the cat's warm fur and looked up at Avery. "How about Oliver?"

The cat raised its head to look at him, and Theo felt judged. "No, huh?"

Avery laughed. "Okay. Kitty has opinions."

"Don't cats always?" Theo said. He gazed at the cat who stared back silently with amber eyes.

"Leonidas." It was a statement, somehow, not a question.

The cat blinked, then resumed purring and settled in for a nap.

"Leonidas it is, then," Theo said. When he glanced up at Avery, the other man had an odd expression on his face. He looked puzzled almost, glancing from Theo to

Leonidas and back, but when he didn't say anything, Theo turned back to the conversation.

"So, I don't count as part of the New Crew? I've only lived here for a few weeks."

"Nah." Avery sat back. His leather jacket squeaked a bit as he stretched his arms overhead. "For one thing you're not a snotty, arrogant, better-than-you sort of person. You're initially a little standoffish, but you clearly have manners and you remember to use them all the time, unlike the New Crew who reserve them only for each other. Second, you live here and not in a soulless box." Avery gestured up at the house, which could honestly use a coat of paint to refresh the siding.

Theo blinked for a moment. *It's probably real wood under that paint, too. Not fiberglass or plastic or something. Huh.*

"And for a third thing? You're Garfield's nephew. He picked you as his heir, which means he thought you'd fit here, and to the folks around here that genuinely care about the area, that means something. That old man was sharp as a tack till the day he died." Avery tipped his head at Theo. "You didn't know him very well, did you?"

"Nope. Just met once for a couple of days when I was a kid." He still thought it was bizarre that Gruncle Garfield had done what he did in his will, but since it felt like the right move for him to be here, he wasn't about to argue.

"You're pretty sharp, too," Avery said. "Not as gregarious or outgoing, though. More guarded and watchful, but I can almost see you fit the puzzle pieces together when you work something out. When Candace dragged that detective into the bar you gave the man a once over and decided immediately that you didn't trust him. He hadn't even opened his mouth."

"Well, what sort of cop wears designer jeans and an

expensive jacket? I promise you he can't afford to dress like that on the paycheck of a civil servant," Theo scoffed.

Avery smirked. "See? You notice things. You seem all quiet and solitary, but you're not, really. You're only quiet until it's time to be loud, I think, and you're far from solitary. I think you're going to be good for the area, and I'm glad we can be friends."

Theo blinked at him. He didn't want to think about how he had come here specifically to be solitary and yet he had still somehow managed to make friends–sort of–with his neighbor, with the Cardosos, with the staff at the Last Pot. Even the grumpy one who now started making his drink before he even ordered it. He had a deal worked out with one of the neighborhood kids and the kid's mom was sending him baked goods. And here sat Avery. Right here, on his porch, earlyish on a Sunday morning drinking his coffee and scratching under Leonidas' chin.

Oh hell, he even had a damn cat.

Theo couldn't deal with it right now and emptied the coffee pot into his mug and stood. "Ready to sift through a room full of lord-knows-what?"

14

STILL CLEANING

They set the coffee pot brewing again–Theo suspected he would need the stuff before too long– and headed into the library or den or whatever you wanted to call it. The small room that looked out onto the back yard and the river beyond, on the back of what Theo thought of as the living room. Leonidas, who had darted inside after them in the manner of cats by almost tripping Theo, had disappeared into the house.

"First day I got here the dust was so thick in the living room that I could track Gruncle Garfield's usual path through it all in the narrow bit of clean floor, all the way back here." Theo sighed. "I just opened all the windows and went after the room with a duster to cope with the worst of it, then proceeded to ignore the whole mess, so I guess I'm not much better."

He stood just inside the door of the library and surveyed the stacks of books and other bits and pieces that were strewn about the room. A desk that looked like it rarely saw use had stacks of books and other detritus piled along the edges with only a small clear space in the middle where a desk lamp sat perched to shine on a small box, which itself sat on a page of notes. There was a well-worn chair by the window overlooking the backyard, and a small table beside it that was overflowing with papers.

A pair of dusty glasses lay on top of the whole mess as if Garfield had just put them down, expecting to be back any moment, and that made Theo stop in the doorway.

"Wow. This is... actually kind of what I expected, to be honest." Avery chuckled from just behind Theo's shoulder, though there was an edge of sadness in the sound. With his punk-rock style and his aqua-colored hair he seemed somehow to fit into the mad scholar's study perfectly

"Garfield was a lot of things, but organized and orderly were never on that list. Man, no wonder Darren liked it over here." Avery stepped over to the bookshelf and blew a cloud of dust off the edge, sneezing almost immediately, then laughing.

"Darren?" Theo eyed the chair before sitting down in it and picking up his great-uncle's glasses.

"My cousin. He and Garfield could get into conversations about the history of this area that would spiral out and lord knows where they'd end up. I'd have to kick them out of the bar at the end of the night sometimes because they'd gotten so deep into their conversation that they forgot where they were." Avery laughed again at the memory, this time sounding a little happier. "I'll admit, I kind of miss the old guy. He was fun, even when he spiraled down one of his research rabbit holes."

"I'm sorry I didn't get to know him better." Theo stepped over to the chair and picked up the glasses, idly wiping the lenses clean with the bottom of his shirt. "I only remember him from a few days when I was a kid. He seemed like a pretty cool guy to me, but my mom thought he was just a crazy old man. She really didn't like him."

Theo held the glasses up to the sunlight filtering through the window and winced. Wow, the old man must have been nearly blind. He put the glasses on the windowsill and turned back to the room.

"Yeah? And she was family? His family, I mean," Avery asked. He wandered over to a stack of books in the corner, grabbed one of the dust rags Theo had brought in last night, and started wiping down the covers. "She was the one related to Garfield, not your father?"

Theo sighed and gingerly sat back down in the chair. He started picking up all the notes, noticing that they were a random assortment of torn-out notebook pages, yellow pad pages, scraps of printer paper, and at least three napkins, one of which had a questionable stain in the corner.

"No. He was my dad's uncle, but I guess he and my grandfather didn't get along so Dad never saw him much. Then he moved out here and that was that. But when I was a kid, we'd take these road trips to important historical or scientific sites. Go camping nearby. I remember Mom sitting me down when we were heading out that year and talking about all the places we were going to visit. You know, The Paleontology Center and the Deschutes Historical Museum, and all that stuff."

Theo reached out and brushed his fingers over the books on the table. "She said that we were going to go camping, but first we were going to visit the museum over at the college, and since he was here, we would stay with Dad's uncle. She warned me that he was a bit eccentric, and not to expect much in the way of education outside the museum, regardless of the fact that this was a college town."

Theo shook his head at the memory he hadn't thought of for decades. "I don't think she was expecting him to be quite *so* odd, though. And I know she was stunned by the number of books he had on every conceivable subject. We were supposed to stay here for a week before heading off to go camping, but she hustled us out of here after only about four days."

Avery stacked another book onto the clean pile next to him. "Why didn't she like him?"

"I think he made her really uncomfortable. She's a very logical, science-minded person. Hates charlatans and liars and is not a fan of stage magicians, so when he started showing me some party tricks–card tricks and sleight-of-hand with coins. You know, things that would entertain any kid. She kind of freaked out a bit."

"Wow." Avery started pulling books off the nearby shelf and chuckled, making a new pile of papers and another one of random small objects, wiping the books down as he pulled them off. "Yeah, I can't see this being a fun place for someone who aggressively disbelieves in magic. Why is that, do you think? I mean, why be so adamant?"

Theo shrugged, watching Avery move for a moment. When the shelf was cleared off, Avery started neatly restoring the books to the shelf, fitting most of the books he had dusted onto it, then started the process again with the next shelf up.

"She's a chemist. Well, she was a chemist professionally until she decided to stay home and raise me. I think she wanted more kids, too, but that never happened. She started teaching at the community college when I was in high school and a bit more independent." Theo shrugged and turned back to his area. He found a teacup under a fallen sheaf of papers, but on top of a stack of books, the stain left by the dregs of a long-gone liquid still in the bottom. There was also a half of a robin's egg and what Theo thought was a cicada wing. He held it up.

"A friend of mine in elementary school found one of these in a park when Mom took us and was showing everyone the 'fairy wing' he found. I remember Mom spent what felt like forever lecturing us both about insects, and we ended up at the library looking up cicadas instead of playing outside for the rest of the afternoon."

Avery scrunched his face up. "Ew, that's awful," he said. "I mean, leaving aside the gruesome idea of fairies somehow losing their wings in a way that some kid would find them, which is frankly a terrifying thought. But to crush a kid's imagination like that. Deliberately and actively destroy it? Sorry, I know she's your mom and all, but that's horrible."

Theo shrugged, though there was a quiet, hidden bit of him that agreed. "She wanted to make sure we understood the real world. It's not like we're likely to get swept off to fairyland, after all," Theo pointed out. "And she was a wonderful mother. Just not into fiction so much."

"Well, no. The portals are closed for the most part. No trips to fairyland for anyone these days, not even for folks who came from there. But still. Storytelling is an intrinsic part of sentient life. There's no rule that says you have to pick an appreciation for fiction *or* an appreciation for science." Avery cleared the next shelf and turned to the stack of books at his elbow to start wiping them down and putting them away. "Taking the belief in magic away from children is just cruel. Who knows what that kid could have grown up to be? Maybe he would have been the next J.R.R. Tolkien? Or Jim Henson? But now his mind is full of facts about cicadas instead of dreams about fairies."

"Portals? You mean like mushroom fairy rings?" Theo snorted. Figures Avery would believe that sort of thing.

"But you're right, I guess. I never thought about it like that. She was just trying her best to prepare us for the real world, is how I looked at it. Would I rather have been allowed to go watch popular movies with my friends? Sure. Or check out the kid's fiction section at the library? Absolutely. But I really liked the archaeology and space documentaries we watched instead. And there were plenty of neat things in the non-fiction section at the library."

Theo frowned at the thing he had just picked up to realize it was a cork tied to a bit of silver tinsel.

"I've never seen a fairy ring that took anyone anywhere. Although, I suppose it must have happened at least a few times for the story to stick, don't you? Anyway, I'm sure your mother was doing her best. It just seems..." Avery shook off his thought. "What would you have been if you hadn't gotten steered away from imagination?" Avery asked.

A memory flashed through Theo's head of one of his teachers in high school beaming at a short story he wrote for class. It was a required class and a required piece of fiction writing, otherwise he would not likely have written it, even though Theo remembered the ideas he used in the story had been kicking around his mind for a while. His teacher had pressed him to try submitting the story to the local literary magazine, but he had decided to submit an article he wrote on global warming instead, thus sending him on his current path.

"She always encouraged me." Theo shrugged and glanced out the window. Then he turned and eyed Avery for a long moment, deciding to trust him. Avery had, after all, let Theo know in a very confidently offhanded way. "A lot of kids like me aren't so lucky."

Avery frowned and shelved the book he had just finished wiping. "Kids like you?"

Theo nodded slowly. "Not entirely straight."

A small line appeared between his eyebrows. "Not entirely... you said your ex was a woman?"

Theo shrugged, the confusion familiar, and answered dryly. "Bisexual is a thing, you realize."

"Oh, I'm aware." Avery grinned. "I just wanted to make sure I understood. I find that when people are making confessions, being sure you understand the confession clearly is important. I'm glad your mom—both your parents, I guess—were supportive."

Theo nodded. "Yeah. She never gave me even a hint of disappointment when I was so nervous and scared about the whole thing. And she loved to talk about archaeology and mummies with me. She never minded when I went on forever about this dig or that discovery, and a lot of the adults around me got visibly bored by it all, even my history teachers. So I'll cut her a lot of slack when it comes to her preferences for science and fact-based reading material."

Avery nodded. "That's great. And I'm really glad you got that support." He took a breath and scrunched up his nose. "But crushing a child's imagination isn't very scientific. And there is a lot of very scientific research out there on imagination and imaginative play and how important it is. Everything from neuroscience to psychology and sociology. Discounting magic just because it hasn't been dissected in a lab is silly, and discrediting imagination just because she doesn't like fiction stories is like cutting off her nose to spite her face."

"What?" Theo blinked at Avery. Somehow this whole conversation had gone running away without him. Weren't they just talking about... "I mean, I know all that, but... what?"

Avery put his rag down and turned to face Theo.

"Well, without imagination, how is anyone supposed to think up the next great experiment? Or come up with a crazy plan to send scientists to Mars? Or figure out a cure for cancer? Yes, those all require a lot of hard facts and repeatable experimentation, but to begin with, to even *start* any of that you have to have solid imagination coupled with a driving curiosity. You have to have *belief*. That's something that almost every kid out there is born with."

"I suppose," Theo agreed. "But that's a different thing than waving around an insect wing and claiming it's from an imaginary creature, no matter how pretty it is."

"First, I disagree. I think it's exactly the same thing. And second..." He peered at Theo now, his eyes narrow and assessing. "Who says fairies are imaginary?"

Theo blinked. "You believe in fairies?"

"Of course I do. It would be a bit hypocritical if I didn't."

Theo looked up at Avery and frowned. "Wait, you're serious. You really believe in tiny human-shaped creatures with wings and magic and the clothes made out of leaves, that sprinkle glittering magic dust everywhere they go."

Avery rolled his eyes. "I mean actual fairies. Yes, with wings and magic. They're not all that tiny though, and their clothes are made out of the same stuff ours is. Well, I guess there are a few hippie sorts, and they probably wear hemp clothes which is sorta like being made out of leaves, I guess, but I don't think that's what you meant."

Theo frowned. "What are you talking about?"

"Fairies." Avery raised his eyebrow, and the silver piercing in the one seemed to wink at Theo. "They're the same size we are. Okay, they do tend to stay on the shorter side of the spectrum, but they're measured in feet and inches just like you and me."

"There's no such thing as fairies, and I don't care what James Barrie has to say on the matter." Theo frowned.

Avery snorted. "No, despite the fun parts of Peter Pan, Mr. Barrie didn't know what he was talking about, but that's a completely different question. Look. I'm not about to go opening your eyes to a whole new world here. That's not the sort of thing that you just dump on a person when you have to go to work in"—he checked his watch—"half an hour. But I'd say that your mom managed to close your mind to an awful lot of the world, simply by declaring it fanciful and unscientific. You need to open your mind and your eyes, Theo. This is an ideal place to do it, here in Greenwoods."

"You're trying to convince me that fairies are real? I don't believe in fairies," Theo said. He couldn't begin to understand what Avery was trying to prove. He snorted a laugh. "Do we need to start clapping and save a life now because I said that?"

Avery sighed. "This isn't a clap-your-hands sort of moment. Nobody dies if you say you don't believe. Again, Peter Pan isn't the be-all and end-all of fairy information. I'm just saying that your mom didn't do you any favors by closing you off to the less lab-based aspects of the world, even if she was wonderful and supportive when you came out to her."

"My mom just pointed out that living in a fantasy world was counter-productive. It's better to stay ground-ed," Theo argued. "She wanted to make sure that I had a firm foundation and a good life."

"Your mom closed minds. Yours, apparently, and your 'fairy wing'-collecting friend in all likelihood. And prob-ably others. When you were a kid, did you want to read a science textbook or an adventure comic? Did you want to watch a documentary on TV after school or did you want to watch cartoons?" Avery frowned slightly as Leonidas picked his way into the room, sniffing delicately and investigating the piles they had created. "Stories and fairy tales are common for any culture, and it's even more important when you're a kid. Your mom sounds like she actively tried to cut you off from that, which would have alienated you from the other kids."

Theo's stomach twisted, remembering how fewer and fewer kids showed up to his birthday parties over the years, how he didn't get invited to go play at their houses after a while. Which was kind of awful, since those were the only times he got to watch TV for fun rather than enrichment. Once he grew past the age educational public TV aimed at, Avery had hit the nail right on the head. It was all documentaries.

"She was getting me ready for adulthood. That's the goal of every parent," Theo protested, but even he could hear how weak his words sounded. His childhood had grown increasingly lonely as he was cut off from his peers by a lack of understanding of pop culture.

"She was cutting you off from the magic of the world. Not all magic is, well, *magic*, after all." A wide grin crept over Avery's face. "But a lot of it is."

"Regardless of my mother's parenting techniques or my grounding in pop culture, magic still isn't real," Theo argued.

"You sure about that?" Avery asked. He reached out and held up a small bottle. The clear glass shone dully, covered in dust as it was, but the contents seemed to swirl and fold over on itself with a golden glow layered through it. "This house seems to be packed with magic. You just have to open your mind to see it."

15

ONE THING AFTER ANOTHER

Theo blinked at the bottle, enchanted by the seemingly independent movement of the liquid inside. It didn't seem that Avery was shaking the bottle or anything like that, the golden liquid churning slowly on its own.

"So…" His voice felt dry and he cleared his throat before continuing. "So, you found a glitter bottle. Penny used to have one that she used to help her calm down when she was really angry. It's pretty, but it proves nothing."

"It's a wealth charm, I think. I could ask Fitz about it. It's magic, though—I can feel it easily. I'm not making that stuff move, there's no way I'm swinging it enough to swirl the liquid around inside like that. It's the magic that stirs it."

"Avery, there's no such thing as magic. Just like there's no such thing as fairies." Theo had regained his mental footing and was getting irritated now.

Avery sighed. "I don't want to believe that you're hopeless, Theo. I won't believe it, but if proof is the only thing that you'll believe in..."

Much to Theo's shock, Avery reached behind his head and had just started to tug off his T-shirt when the phone in his leather jacket rang. Avery grunted and let the fabric fall back into place.

"God, the timing is amazing as always." He fished the phone from the jacket and answered. "Yeah. What? ... Shit. I'll be right there."

He frowned as he grabbed up his jacket and settled the leather on his shoulders. "There's been tags appearing all through the whole neighborhood, ending at the bar, where some idiot driver proceeded to stare so hard at one of the tags that he ran the red light at the corner and caused a three-car pileup that slammed into the building."

"Oh, shit. Is everyone okay?" Theo forgot about the argument for a moment. "Is the bar okay?"

"I guess I'll find out. We're going to be closed tonight for sure though. I'll let you know what's up. Sorry I have to duck out." Avery grimaced. "I'll, um...I'll show you later, though. If you still need your proof." He reached out and scratched the cat behind the ears for a moment, then with a nod he was gone.

A few seconds later, Theo heard the front door open and close, and he was left with his mind spinning madly. What the hell proof could Avery possibly have that required nudity?

His brain helpfully supplied a description in one of the books Penny had left lying around. It was a paranormal romance where the aggressive, overbearing leading male had ripped off his clothes before turning into a giant wolf and rescuing the simpering female lead from...something. Theo didn't remember what and didn't much care.

The explanation given was that the clothes would get

in the way of his transformation since they wouldn't change with him. *Rather shortsighted magic,* Theo had thought before he put the book down again. Unusually for him, the fantasy elements hadn't irritated him so much in the scene as the abrasive "alpha" character's personality did.

Leonidas jumped into his lap, startling him out of the memory, purring loud enough he was surprised the window next to him didn't rattle, and settled down comfortably. Theo chuckled and started running his hand over the cat's fur, surprisingly clean and soft for a stray.

Theo sat back in the overstuffed chair where he had been sorting things and growled at the papers he had collected. The books in the room covered all sorts of disconnected subjects: history, city planning, chemistry, some sort of medical text in German, a book of watercolor botanical prints in French.

There were coins and more feathers and twigs and random things with no rhyme or reason that Theo could figure out. The old man had been eccentric, that much was obvious. Probably nuts, too, given the randomness of the bits and bobs that weren't books or notes.

Well, no that wasn't fair. He couldn't blame a dead man for his current mood. It wasn't Great-uncle Garfield's fault that he had unintentionally taken sides. Theo could still hear his mother's comment, all those months ago, when he told her that Garfield McCann was dead.

"That old man was delusional and I feel responsible for not getting him the help he needed. Believing in magic and supernatural nonsense and trying to drag the whole family into it all. Poor man had lost his mind entirely. *Magic,*" she had said.

The derision she had put into that last word had surprised Theo. She practically spat it out. He knew his mother didn't approve of, well, of imagination if he was being entirely honest with himself—not that he intended to tell Avery that again—but she had sounded almost angry at the whole idea. "At least you have a solid footing in the *real* world. You've got real talent, baby, and you write about real things. Not that... intellectually bankrupt garbage."

He had always known that she didn't like fairy tales or fantasy stories even though he did, and Dad didn't seem to have an opinion. Theo had thought it was odd, but it was also just *Mom* to him. He never thought there was anything sinister about it. Everyone had opinions and likes and dislikes. Avoiding popular comic books and young adult fiction stories seemed like a small enough price to pay to make his mother happy.

He thought of his mother's unflagging support for him when he came to her, tearful and worried that something was wrong with him because he was different than some of the other boys who had been talking after gym class. Mom had simply sighed and sat him down to explain that science hadn't fully explored the neurological origins of sexuality but it was an undeniable fact that there were as many variations in that aspect of humanity as there were eye colors, and then she had discussed gender a bit, in case that was relevant as well. It wasn't for Theo, but it certainly helped him in college.

It had been weirdly reassuring that she didn't care at all. So long as there was some sort of scientific footing she could find for it, she was unflappable. She loved him, in her own way, and he had always known that if he had a problem he could go to her to find a solution. She'd been a great mom. Avery had never met her and simply didn't know what he was talking about.

His eyes drifted to the bottle Avery had shown him. It sat on top of the stack of books that the other man had been halfway through wiping off and restoring to the bookshelf, the liquid inside still swirling around the glass as it sat undisturbed.

Theo sank back into the chair and let his head fall back. Avery was already a much better friend than Jerry had ever been, the lying bastard. Before they even really talked, Avery had jumped to Theo's defense when Candace dragged that detective into the bar. Jerry probably would have excused himself to go take a call or something, leaving Theo to deal with it all alone and just never come back. Hell, even Penny would have excused herself until the whole scene was over. Or, Theo laughed quietly to himself, maybe she would have grabbed Jerry for a quickie while Theo was dealing with it all.

On the other hand... Avery was insistent in his belief in magic. It sounded insane, but Avery just stated it like it was pure fact, as if commenting that the traffic was bad lately or that rain is wet. When Theo scoffed, Avery had actually looked hurt, which made Theo feel like a total asshole. So what if the man believed in magic and fairies and whatever else? He was a good man and he cared about the people around him. That much was clear, and Theo was starting to wonder if that was more important than a "firm grounding in reality," as his mother would say. Penny and Jerry had been firmly grounded in reality and look how that worked out.

Theo blinked around him, his eyes landing on the half-filled bookshelf and all the books that were neatly dusted and carefully put away. Avery didn't push Theo to do anything, aside from opening his mind to another way of thinking. He snorted and rolled his eyes at himself for thinking that if opening his mind wound up involving Avery shirtless, then it wasn't all that bad. Maybe he had a tattoo he wanted to show off? That would make sense, if he thought that somehow a tattoo would prove something.

It would in a novel, probably. Maybe a tattoo that moved, or shimmered or something, but if he were writing this in a book, he would...

Leonidas stretched, resettled, and purred louder in his lap.

Theo frowned at the papers strewn around the space in front of him without seeing them. Was that what he wanted? To write a book that wasn't about politics or science? A memory flickered through his mind of an idea that had come to him while he daydreamed his way through several of his classes in high school. An idea that his mother had discouraged in favor of another which had, in all fairness, set him up as a successful writer of science and archaeology for the layman. But still...

The screech of tires trying to stop and the immediate crunching of a car folding in on itself jerked Theo out of his whirling thoughts and he stood, dislodging the cat, who protested loudly. He ran to the front window and peered out to see a delivery van around ten feet shy of the stop sign at the corner, and a dark gray sedan crushed up to the van's back bumper. There were bits of plastic strewn across the pavement and steam or smoke wafting out from under the sedan's hood.

"Shit," Theo muttered and grabbed a jacket as he dashed out the door.

"Holy shit, did you see that thing?" The van driver was slowly sliding out of his seat, looking unsteady but mostly okay. The sedan driver was still mostly hidden behind the deflating airbag, though, so Theo hurried over the driver's side door. He knocked on the window.

"Hey, you okay?"

A hand batted down the fabric of the airbag and Stacy Cardoso peered blearily up at him.

"I'm going to open the door, okay?" Theo called and

she nodded slowly. Theo opened the door gently and put a hand on her arm in case she wasn't feeling stable.

"Thank goodness for seatbelts and stuff, huh?" she mumbled. "But hoo boy, I'm gonna hurt in the morning."

"I bet you are. How're you feeling right now, anything broken? Any cuts or anything?" Theo asked.

"Did you *see* that *thing?*" The van driver stumbled up to them. "Oh, man, lady I am so sorry, you okay? But holy shit, what *was* that thing? It was *huge!* Where the hell did it go?" He looked around wildly.

"I..." Stacy frowned and seemed to be assessing herself. "I think I'm okay. Bruised to hell and back, I bet, but nothing feels like it's broken or anything. I think I can get out."

"Okay. If you need to lean on me, go right ahead. Should I call Jorge? He gave me his number for when I had your son come mow my lawn, just in case."

"Would you, please?"

Theo gave her an arm to lean on as she slowly stepped out of her car. The van driver followed, still going on about whatever "that thing" was and if they'd seen it. Theo hadn't and he didn't think Stacy was even listening to the question. The sound of a siren drawing close caused him to glance up, and when he did, he noticed the paint dripping down the face of the stop sign, an acid blue against the bright red.

The squiggly tag seemed to shimmer for a second before the police car turned the corner, the siren deafening this close. With a final "whoop", the noise blessedly died, and Stacy stopped cringing where she sat on the curb next to Theo.

"Does anyone need medical treatment?" the cop called out of the door he had just opened.

Theo glanced at Stacy, who was leaning harder on him

and he nodded. "Definitely, at least a check over, I'm afraid." He turned back to her. "I know ambulances are stupid expensive, but you need to get looked at."

"S'okay. We have savings," she answered, slurring a little which made Theo worry about how hard she had banged her head into the airbag.

"And they have family," Ivette added. Theo tried not to jump at her sudden appearance.

"I didn't even see you come out," he said. He glanced at the van driver who was now trying to explain to the officer that some "giant thing" had jumped out in front of his van which is why he stopped short.

Ivette sighed. "It is getting worse. Whoever it is that is painting these glyphs either doesn't know or doesn't care what damage they are causing."

Theo blinked up at her. "Glyphs?"

Ivette smiled down at him, and he idly noticed that her twinset today was a cheerful bright peach, like a sunset. It was oddly soothing. "You have a lot to learn, young Theo. Don't worry. You will have help."

"Another gut feeling?" Theo felt one eyebrow rise up his forehead.

Ivette smiled and winked, then she turned to glide over to where the van driver was waving wildly and talking about whatever it was he saw that caused him to stop short. He heard her start talking to the officer, presenting herself as a witness.

16

TROUBLE COMES IN THREES

Theo slumped down in the chair in the waiting room and leaned his head back on the wall. Waiting sucked. He tried to summon some zen, but the harsh lighting and the smell of disinfectant and bad coffee was too aggressive. He couldn't do anything about the smell, but he could close his eyes and try not to groan.

Two hours after the accident and they were still grinding their way through the routine of hospital administrative nonsense and testing. Stacy was probably fine, but it always took so long to get through everything at a hospital, even in an emergency room. She had asked him to stay with her in the ambulance, so they had let him ride along. Jorge was with the kids, and he had said that as soon as he could get someone to sit with them he would be there. Theo had promised he would stay until then. It wasn't a problem, honestly. He had nowhere else to be and being there for some people who seemed like they were turning into actual friends felt damn good, but man. Hospital waiting rooms were terrible.

"These seats are almost as uncomfortable as the ones at the precinct. I'm honestly impressed."

Shit.

"Coffee is probably just as good too. Did you need something, Detective?" Theo didn't bother opening his eyes. He was tired and frustrated and worried about what seemed like all his friends here and his patience was extremely thin.

"Yes. I need you to answer a few questions, finally," Angelo said. He wasn't even bothering with his good-cop voice. This was the "talking to a suspect" voice.

"Don't you need to read me my Miranda Rights before you start in on the interrogation?"

"Do I need to arrest you before you answer any questions? I've been trying to ask you a few questions for days now, and you have deliberately avoided me. Honestly, it doesn't make you look very innocent."

"I did answer your questions. I can't help it that you won't accept those answers," Theo replied. He rolled his eyes behind his eyelids which only made his head start to ache.

"What answers? The vague statement that you don't know anything? Your total refusal to acknowledge that it is extremely suspicious that you move here at precisely the same time that all this starts up?" Angelo's tone held accusations that he was holding back. "Why is it that you won't tell me what I want to know?"

"You've been following me for a week," Theo said with a tired sigh. "Surely you have enough surveillance to know that I had nothing to do with this. I honestly don't know why you're so interested in me other than Candace's insistence that I am involved. You think none of us have noticed you talking to Marielle so often?"

"And what's wrong with Ms. Trevor?" Angelo asked. "She, at least, has been forthcoming and very helpful."

"Oh, I bet she has." Theo rolled his head to blink his eyes open and look at the detective.

"Who else are you watching? We've noticed the patrol cars sweeping by the Cardoso's place. And Avery's very much over having the 'plumbing van' sitting across the street from his place. Christ, you've even had someone watching Anton Jones and the man is almost seventy! All people that Marielle has been trying to drive out of the neighborhood." Theo started ticking his list off on his fingers. "I told her off for bullying children. Avery and Darren have the audacity to live together and Avery dates men. How horrible. The Cardosos are clearly far too brown to live near Marielle, and the only reason she leaves Ivette alone is because Ivette could buy and sell Marielle and not even notice the difference to her bank account. Poor Mr. Jones is just an avid gardener, and has been since he moved into that house almost fifty years ago."

He took a breath to calm down. Getting wound up wasn't going to help anything.

"The only reason you're here is because Marielle Trevor didn't like being reminded that she's not Queen of Whitelake and sent one of her lackeys to yank your leash. Why the hell would I paint over a stop sign? In front of my own house? Not that apparently that had a damn thing to do with it. Dude was going on about seeing something run into the road, but I was a bit busy taking care of my friend to worry about him." Theo growled.

His patience was very thin at this point and he was worried about his friend. Did she count as a friend? She had sent over brownies and had sent a huge thermos of lemonade for her son to share when he came over to mow the lawn with Holly, and then she had stopped by and talked for a bit when he was sitting on his porch a few times and she was jogging.

Artie had also cheerfully chatted with him when he took a break from the lawn work, and Jorge and Abe had joined them when he came by to check on his son's progress. The whole family was friendly. Did that mean they were friends? Just neighbors? Friendly neighbors?

He had moved here to get away from people and live quietly and now, it seemed, he had more of a social life than he had before the breakup. At least these people were *his* friends. He thought. Probably? Stacy wanted him to stay when she was in trouble and he was worried about her, and he would just leave it at that for now.

The last thing he needed was a snotty, arrogant cop harping at him. This day had been shitty enough already, thanks.

"I'm here because the vandalism and the accidents are linked somehow. I am also here because your arrival at approximately the same time as the vandalism started is one hell of a coincidence."

"Well, I got here when I got here and didn't even know about any of it until Marielle Trevor showed up on my porch, weeks later, uninvited, and tried to insinuate herself into my house."

"Is there a reason you don't want her in your house?" Detective Angelo asked. He leaned his elbows on his knees and tipped his head at Theo.

Theo almost laughed at the obvious attempt at a "good-cop" technique. The man was trying to sound friendly and look unimposing this round, and for some reason, the whole thing struck Theo as entertaining.

"Yes," he said. "Because I don't like her. I have the very strange personal habit of not wanting people I dislike and don't trust in my home."

"You invited Mr. Cardoso in the other day," he said mildly.

Theo just raised his eyebrow and met the detective's gaze. "And I didn't invite you, either. If you're feeling slighted over it, then you're a better detective than I thought."

"Something very odd is going on over in the Greenwoods neighborhood, something bigger than just vandalism, and I would like you to help me figure it out, Mr. Warren. All those people you just mentioned are keeping secrets. Even Mr. Jones. You're new to the area, so as I said in the first place, you might notice things that long-time residents haven't," Detective Angelo said. He was trying very hard to sound reasonable but wasn't doing a very good job. "I don't see any reason why we can't work together to sort out what is going on over there. If you're not involved in this vandalism, then help me find out who is. It's escalating, and it's somehow tied to a number of muggings and traffic accidents in the area. Isn't the safety and well-being of your neighbors important to you?"

"People are allowed their privacy, Detective."

Angelo gestured around the room, implying that it must be important to Theo or he wouldn't be sitting in a hospital waiting for Stacy to finish getting the X-rays taken. "Don't you want to make sure that your neighborhood is safe and the wrong element is removed from the area? I spoke to Mrs. Trevor–"

"The 'wrong element,' Detective?" A flash of rage shot through Theo. "Have you investigated Marielle? Nobody has noticed any patrol cars outside *her* house day and night. No, but heaven help us if someone *brown* lives next door. And the blameless Mrs. Trevor can't *possibly* be expected to live anywhere that she might be exposed to a man with a piercing or two that goes on a date with another man, am I right? It might offend her very delicate sensibilities and destroy the moral fiber of the neighborhood, and indeed, the country! Forget the fact that the Cardoso family has lived in this area for generations and Jorge is a respected and sought after architect, or that Avery moved here are least five years before that shrew did and has been a friendly fixture in the area ever since. The only thing odd going on in my neighborhood community is that the people actually seem to want to be, I don't know... what's the word? Oh. *A community.* And we don't appreciate dictators moving in and trying to take over and maliciously trying to drive out anyone that doesn't fall in line with an incredibly Victorian view of *the natural order.*"

Detective Angelo blinked in surprise.

"What? What are you talking about? Ms. Trevor said—"

"I don't give a damn what *Ms. Trevor* said." Theo was officially over it. The not-quite argument with Avery, the revelation that maybe he didn't have his life quite as sorted as he had thought, the accident, the worry for his...screw it, his friend Stacy... He had exactly no patience left for an over-moneyed cop who thought Marielle and her lackeys were anything approaching accurate in their reporting. "I am exhausted, I am stressed out, I am worried about my friend–who, I might add, is one of the *'wrong element'* that Marielle is trying to drive off–I've been mugged, harassed, argued with one of my closest friends, and now I've been sitting in this damn hospital waiting room for hours. You want to talk to me, *Detective*, you can call my lawyer. I have nothing more to say to Marielle's pet cop."

"What?" Detective Angelo blinked. He seemed genuinely taken aback, but Theo was past caring about the man.

Theo glared back. Angelo looked worn out, his eyes

dark from exhaustion and his shoulders drooping. He was wearing another pair of designer jeans, though he had no jacket this time. His expensive tie loosened and the sleeves on his tailored shirt rolled up his forearms, he actually looked a bit rumpled. Like a young, wealthy Columbo. For a moment, Theo softened at the signs of a long, sleepless night followed by another day of hard work. Detective Angelo was nothing if not dedicated.

It just made Theo even more wary of the man, and considering how angry he was, "wary" wasn't a feeling he had expected to layer into his emotional state, yet here he was. Columbo's success had hinged on his deceptively harmless rumpled-ness, after all.

"I am not interested in assisting that arrogant, manipulative woman in any manner whatsoever, not even if it's through someone else. I've had enough of that toxic garbage in my life. I just got rid of it all, and I won't invite it back in. Not to mention the fact that I am fully aware of how much it costs to buy a pair of Balenciaga jeans." Theo glanced pointedly down at said jeans, noting then ignoring the stains on the knees and the dust on the cuffs.

"I don't even need to look up the public records for local municipal salaries to know that there's no chance of that happening on a cop's paycheck." Theo leaned closer to the startled man. "So why don't you take yourself and your leash back to Marielle? I don't have any more time for you."

"Mr. Warren? Mrs. Cardoso is back from X-ray if you would like to go sit with her again." The nurse's timing was amazing, though by the way she bit her lip and the sparkle in her eye, Theo guessed she had heard at least a little of the exchange. He stood and followed her, leaving the detective sputtering in the waiting room.

"That was the most impressive verbal takedown I have

ever heard in my life. I think you just made the hospital gossip hall of fame," she said once they were a reasonable distance from the door.

Theo snorted. "Thanks, I think. I probably shouldn't have said any of that, but I'm a bit out of mental energy today, and that guy has always set off alarms for some reason."

"No, sir. Thank you." She grinned and patted his shoulder and turned, her whole body sparkling with mirth, and Theo just sighed and turned to grab the chair to pull it up by the bed. "I'm going to be dining out on that story for weeks! And sometimes you just don't know why you react to a person. You'll sort it out eventually." She patted his shoulder and left the room.

"You okay, Theo?" Stacy asked, her expression strained but a bit worried. Her T-shirt was wrinkled and stretched out of shape and someone had given her a band to tie her hair back with. The bruises on her face from the airbag were starting to turn a really impressive purple.

"Shouldn't I be asking you that? How are you holding up?" Theo propped his elbows on the side of her bed, leaning on them and trying to dredge up a smile.

"I'm sore as hell and they're a bit worried about my ribs, but I'm not. I'll heal. You look like you're trying to decide whether to laugh or cry." She reached out and put her hand over his, where it folded over his other arm.

"Eh. Marielle's pet detective caught up with me in the waiting room, is all. She managed to convince him that I'm involved in the graffiti that's been popping up all over lately, so he's been a pain in my neck for the last few days." Theo shrugged.

Stacy pulled a face. "That woman. Is that why there's been a cop car on our street all the damn time?"

Theo chuckled. "Yeah. I seem to attract the crazies."

He opened his eyes wide and leaned back, making an exaggerated look of suspicion, which made Stacy grin as he intended. "She's sent him after half the neighborhood."

"Ugh. I'm sorry, though. I bet she turned on you because you defended my boys and Mateo I feel responsible that you're now a wanted man." She grinned, but it wasn't as cheerful as he had gotten used to from her.

"Nah, she would have found a reason not to like me sooner or later. I'm not Stepford Neighbor material, in a number of ways." He shrugged. "I also went and made friends with Avery and Ivette. I am clearly irredeemable."

"Stepford Neighbor. I like it." She nodded. Then she frowned and tipped her head slightly in thought. "But why would the detective come here, though?"

Theo sighed and rolled his eyes. "The stop sign was tagged, so he connected some dots. It was also right outside my house, and he seems to think that the graffiti and the bad traffic are connected somehow. Ivette agreed, sort of, I guess? I have no idea."

"Do I remember Ivette coming out and saying something about glyphs?"

Theo groaned. "Yeah, I think that's what she said. I wasn't exactly worried about Ivette at that point, I was more worried about you."

"Aww, you do care!" she teased.

"Well, of course I do!" Theo frowned. "I admit that I'm not all that good with people, but I'm not heartless. I even feel bad about going off at the damn detective, even though he pushed my buttons hard with that *wrong element* bullshit."

"Oh, honey," Stacy said, tugging on his hand until he looked up at her. "I think you're just fine with people. You stepped right in when you saw a bully harassing some kids, you told Marielle off when she was trying to pull a rank she doesn't actually have. You're polite to Aunt Ivette and she doesn't compliment many people on their manners. You sat with me when I really needed someone to lean on, and you're *still* here. Those are not the actions of someone bad with people."

Theo shrugged again. "My mom may not have encouraged much in the way of social customs, but she was very serious about learning basic manners."

Stacy snorted. "Social customs?"

"She really never understood why people got emotional all the time, but she was very good at observing behavior and knowing what to do when." He sighed. "I'm starting to wonder a lot of things about her, to be honest."

"Well, I don't know about her, but from what I know about you, you're just fine with people. A bit awkward sometimes, but not any more than most of us, and I'm really glad you moved here. I'm glad to know you." She smiled at him, and it was a very maternal expression, even with the black eyes and hint of pain in her movements.

"Thanks." Theo knew he was blushing. At least his ears were hot.

"Besides, it would be boring as hell to be here in the hospital all alone," she said with a smirk.

"Oh, I see. You just like me for a distraction."

"Of course! Now tell me what Ivette said about the stop sign."

Theo frowned and tried to remember. He had no idea why it was important, but she asked, and it was as good as any other topic to pass the time.

17

ENOUGH ALREADY

Theo had barely closed the door behind him after returning from the hospital, when his phone rang. Stacy was going to be very sore and needed to take it easy but was otherwise fine, thankfully. About the only thing that was looking positive for him at this point. He had argued with Avery, hadn't gotten half as much done with the cleanup as he wanted to, then basically watched his friend get injured and helped her the hospital where he had thrown insults at a police detective who, while irritating as hell was only doing his job. An A-plus day, really.

Groaning, he fumbled in his pocket and wandered into the living room. It was still dusty and cluttered. The bit of mess he and Avery had started cleaning was spilling through the door from the back library, but at least there was a sofa to sit on and that was immensely appealing after so many hours in those terrible hospital chairs. Definitely not how he had expected to end his day.

"Hi Mom," he said once he accepted the call. "What's up? It's been a hell of a day so far."

"Oh? What happened? Is everything okay?" she asked. The concern in her voice that hinted that she was already sorting out logistics if she needed to come out and help made Theo smile. As irritating as the woman was, he knew he could count on her when he needed to.

"Eh. I'm fine, Mom, and so is everyone else mostly. My neighbor was in a car accident right in front of the house and was pretty badly shaken up, so I stayed with her until her husband could get to the hospital. She's got a few bruised ribs and some nasty bruises on her face and shoulder from the airbag and seatbelt, but it looks like she's fine otherwise. No concussion, just a headache. The other guy was fine, too, I think. But I didn't see him after we got into the ambulance. He was up and moving around on his own, though, so he's probably okay."

Theo slumped into the sofa cushions and decided that the thing was actually pretty comfortable. Maybe he should figure out a way to get it cleaned instead of removed. Put a television in here and it would be a nearly perfect room.

"Oh. I was concerned that you needed help. I mean, I'm glad your neighbor is not badly injured, poor driving is so dangerous, after all. Are you sure you're okay, sweetheart?"

"Yeah. But those hospital chairs are pretty awful. I just got home and I'm very excited about this sofa at the moment. I need to get it cleaned, though, it's dusty," he said. "There was also a pileup near the Three-Legged Wolf—that local bar I like? A car hit the building, I understand, but I don't know more than that yet."

"How frightening!" She clucked sympathetically then moved immediately on to scolding him. "Well, since you're perfectly well, then maybe you can explain to me why your agent called me this morning because she couldn't get a hold of you. I am not your answering service, Theo."

He sighed and rubbed his free hand over his eyes. "I know Mom. I just haven't been in a position to answer when she calls. Her timing has been amazing recently, and then when I do get a free moment all I want is to sit in the peace and quiet, so I forget." He didn't actually think that would put his mother off. Sure enough, he heard another *tsk* over the phone.

"There is no excuse for rudeness, Theobold, I raised you better than that. Especially rudeness in a professional situation. She said he has been trying to get hold of you for several days now," she said. "Apparently there is a meeting of some sort, some kind of conference, and they want you to speak on the article you wrote about the dig at Saqqara. The one you are basing your book around."

Theo sighed. He knew. He had listened to Abby's voicemails. If he was going to be honest, he had been avoiding her calls for exactly that reason. As much as he did love archaeology—and he refused to attribute that to sneaky movie-viewings at a sympathetic neighbor boy's house that featured a certain Nazi-punching archaeology professor—Theo very much did not enjoy public speaking. He had really only been doing it because Penny wanted him to. Had wanted him to "advance his career."

Theo sighed. "There's some fascinating stuff coming out of that dig. Just tons of mummies. Games. So many mummified cats..."

"I know. And, more importantly, so do you. And you know the political climate that those folks are digging in, which is just as important as the artifacts themselves. Which is why you're such an excellent choice for a speaker," she said.

He should have known she wouldn't be distracted.

Mom wanted him to advance his career as well, and she was much harder to deny than Penny.

"I really don't like public speaking, Mom. I'm more of a homebody, you know?" Theo sighed.

"I know, sweetie, but we all have to do hard things sometimes. I know you want to have books out, so this is an important step to getting your name out there. It's a bit of a vicious cycle, I'm afraid. In order to publish, you have to attend the conferences, but if you want to be taken seriously at the conferences you must be published." She sighed now, and the sound was full of regret. "I don't have the skill to write a whole book. Contributing to textbooks is about all I can do."

"That's not true, Mom. You're teaching at the college and tutoring, *and* you're leading those online classes."

"True. That's true," she agreed. "But nobody's asking me to speak at fancy conferences." Mom was not good at teasing, but she was making an effort at least. Theo chuckled at her mild joke.

"They'd be lucky to have you there, and you know it," he said. "They're just intimidated by your terrifying intellect. Don't want to get shown up."

"You're such a sweetheart. I love you too. Call your agent," she said.

"Yes, Mom." He sighed again, then winced and hoped is mother hadn't heard.

"And I do hope your neighbor recovers quickly. Auto accidents are never a fun thing to experience, even when you mostly walk away," she said. "So you're getting out and about, then? Have you made many friends? I assume this woman *is* a friend if you sat with her at the hospital. Or is she more? I suppose if you're putting down roots and making social connections you really aren't coming home."

"She's happily married, Mom. With kids, one of whom is now in charge of my lawn maintenance. I like all four of them, the husband included. They're friends and good neighbors." He was glad she couldn't see him rolling his eyes at her. "And this is my home now."

He needed to get her off this apparent desire to see him coupled at all costs, so Theo told her about Avery and his hair and his protectiveness, and how Theo hadn't managed to meet Avery's cousin yet but wanted to. They talked all about the Cardosos, and their relationship to Ivette next door, and about how Marielle was trying to run them all out for no reasons that he could understand. And about the cat that adopted Theo, and who was, even now, jumping up onto the couch to settle in heavily against Theo's leg. She sympathized and made outraged noises at all the places he expected her to, and agreed that the HOA president sounded like an intolerant twit who shouldn't have any power at all, not even the sliver of authority the HOA seemed to give her.

Finally, it was time to wrap up and she reminded him again to call his agent about the speaking gig.

"It's a good opportunity to get your name further out there, so people will remember you. Name recognition will give you more leverage with a publisher, sweetie," she reminded him. "And lead to more opportunities to present."

"I know, Mom. I'll think about it and call her, okay?"

"Okay. She shouldn't have to call your mother to get hold of you, Theobold." The censure in her tone was both unmistakable and entirely familiar.

"Yes, Mom." Theo nodded even though she couldn't see him.

They hung up, and true to his word, Theo called his agent immediately, explaining that he had been busy with moving and getting settled and then about his friend getting in an accident. Because his mom was right, Stacy and her family were well on the way to being good friends–and wasn't that an odd feeling?–but there was no excuse for blatant rudeness.

After a long conversation with the woman, Theo ended the call after he promised to put a presentation together and had put the conference into his calendar. It meant days of meeting and greeting, one full presentation on the public perception of current Egyptian archaeology in view of the current political climate and how that could relate to funding and public support of ongoing digs, and very probably several panel appearances. He had just over a month to prepare for it and already Theo couldn't wait for it to be over.

He groaned and flopped his head back on the couch, staring at the ceiling and wondered how much more today could throw at him. Moments like this, it felt like his life wasn't his own. He didn't want to attend the damn conference. He didn't want to give talks about... Well, about anything really. He loved reading about archaeology and science, and all the amazing things that people were discovering every day, but...

His phone dinged with a text message, and he glanced down at it.

Avery: *Man, this is a mess. Jorge texted to let me know Stacy's home and doing much better, largely thanks to you. Said he left you a voicemail. You okay?*

Theo: *I didn't really do anything. Just sat with her. But I'm glad she's okay. I was on the phone with my mom, so I missed his call. How's the bar?*

Avery: *Like I said, it's a mess. A truck smashed into the side of the building. There's glass everywhere and bricks all over the ground and the driver has got to have a few broken bones, but he's gone off in an ambulance a while ago. The truck just got hauled off a few minutes ago, though, and now we can see what's left of the building. It's not good.*

Theo winced.

Avery: *We have to put plywood over the hole. Cleanup will take a bit longer. Afraid the Wolf's closed until further notice.*

He ended the message with a scrunched-up frowny face emoji and Theo could hear the frustration in Avery's words.

Theo: *I wish there was something I could do, but I would be more of a hazard on the site than a help.*

Avery: **grinning emoji* No, just stay safe. One of those graffiti tags was painted on the Wolf's window, and it seems to have acted like a target for the truck to hit. Jorge said there was one on the stop sign where the accident was. There's something in the air tonight, and I don't like it. Can I come back there after we're done here? I think we have a lot to talk about, and honestly, my gut is telling me that you're a target.*

Er… well that was odd, but Theo didn't think he'd mind the company tonight.

Theo: *Sure, come on by. Um, I'm sorry I'm so prickly about some stuff.*

Avery: *Don't worry about it. I'm mostly just surprised, is all. We'll talk when I get there. I'll bring beer.*

There wasn't really anything Theo could do other than sympathize. He was no good with tools, and a bit of a hazard at building anything, as he learned during his ill-fated attempt to volunteer at building homes for those who needed them. They had quickly found another way for him to help that kept him far away from the actual construction.

Theo thumbed through his phone and found a gif of a cat-like cartoon critter hugging someone's foot to send in reply. It looked comforting and a little silly so maybe it would make Avery smile.

One of his new friends was laid up. Another was scrambling to literally repair his workplace. His mother was breathing down his neck about work he didn't want to do for a career path he was coming to realize that didn't want to follow quite so zealously, and he was now committed to this stupid conference. Could life get much worse?

Oh, yeah. The police seemed to think he had something to do with all this insane tagging going on around town. Theo was over it. All of it. Someone else could have his life, he wanted to trade it in for something else.

He groaned and glared at Leonidas, who simply blinked back at him with glowing amber eyes.

A pounding on his door a few minutes later had Theo wanting to cry. There was absolutely no way on earth that he wanted to deal with whoever it was on the other side of that bit of wood. Anyone banging on a front door that way was arrogant, pushy, or flat-out rude, or a lovely mixture of all three.

"Theo, I know you're in there, Percy saw you come in when he was jogging by!" Marielle's shrill voice sliced through the door and even the cat shuddered and turned to glare in her direction as if the door wasn't even there. All three it was, then.

"Too bad your glare can't ward off evil," Theo whispered to the cat. One last scratch behind the ears and Theo carefully lifted his new friend to the sofa cushion and stood. "I'm going to sneak out the back. You stay here and hold down the fort, hmm?"

The cat quietly meowed, as if being careful to prevent Marielle from hearing, and settled into the cushion.

Theo grinned. "Best guard cat I've ever been adopted by. Thanks, Leo."

The cat didn't answer, and Theo chuckled to himself. Marielle kept banging on the door and telling him to get the door open and explain himself. She didn't elaborate on what, exactly, needed explaining, or why she thought she had any right to demand he speak to her at all, but that pretty much wrapped her up in a nutshell, as far as Theo thought.

Grabbing his keys and his wallet as quietly as he could from the front table, Theo thanked his lucky stars that the front door was actually solid wood, and not a glorified window like so many were. Nope, just solid walls and an attractive, thick slab of what he guessed was oak or something equally sturdy. He jumped and almost stumbled into the small table when she banged on the door again, but he managed to recover enough to tiptoe to the kitchen and out the back door.

"Theo!"

On the deck, he took a deep breath of the cold evening air. One step closer to peace. He could still hear her, but from the outside the commotion seemed much farther away. A few steps past the shed and he made it to the gate. He grimaced as he went through, still needing to get some paint to try to cover up the graffiti.

Interestingly, it looked like someone had tried to scrub at it already. Some of the lurid red paint was faded, and a corner of the thing was so light as to be almost missing. The ghost of the spray paint was still fairly obvious on the fence's light color anyway, and the whole fence was looking a little tired, so a new paint job wasn't going to hurt anything, but still. It was certainly kind of someone to try to help him with it.

A faint, shrill demand for entry reached him, and Theo

shivered again. The woods across the river looked lovely and peaceful, and he hadn't actually made any time to go hiking since he had moved. Now seemed like an excellent opportunity for an evening stroll. Decision made, Theo headed down the small path to the footbridge that connected the Greenwoods neighborhood to the forest.

18

INTO THE WOODS

T heo sighed in relief when he reached the trees of the forested park on the other side of the river. The trail led under their green branches and offered relief from the loud, gray hurry of the city. Even a drowsy, small-college town heading into spring had a certain energetic bustle to it that vanished here in the darkening woods.

Theo laughed at himself. When was the last time he had been so fanciful? It felt good, though, to let his mind wander and think how it wanted. To not rein in his more off-the-wall ideas because they're not salable to his usual publications.

It was cool in the forest. The trees grew thick and large, which surprised Theo. They were bigger and older than he had been expecting, the tangled undergrowth seeming at once formidable and inviting. His brain flashed back to the mural at the Last Pot, and then to the image of Avery from his dream standing fierce and fae and cloaked in dreamland magic as much as he was in the strange armor.

Theo laughed again, out loud. Greenwoods was

getting into his psyche. Gruncle Garfield would be pleased, Theo mused. That thought immediately brought another: his mother would be horrified. Theo sighed. What the hell was he going to do?

Dusk was falling over the town, which meant that under the shadow of the trees it was now nearly night, but Theo could see clearly enough. There was a moon, beaming down like a floodlight, and the path was clear enough that he wasn't worried about getting lost as he considered what he was doing with his life. There were no turns on the trail, and it seemed to loop pleasantly near enough to the river that Theo caught occasional glimpses of it through the trees, the dusk moonlight sparkling on the surface.

He walked for a while, not really worrying about the time, letting himself sort through the madness of his day, which seemed insanely long in hindsight. The cat moving in, Avery's insistence on magic, the accident at the bar, the accident in front of his house. Stacy and the van's driver and the detective and his mother and Marielle. How had so much *stuff* been packed into one single day? His thoughts and memories of the day swirled through his mind like the glitter in that odd bottle Avery had found earlier, forming ephemeral patterns for a tiny moment before moving again to form a new picture.

It was the sound of voices that caught his attention and brought him blinking back into the present.

"It's too far, Moth! I know you're pissed, but those people had nothing to do with it!" Whoever was speaking wasn't sure of themselves in the least–their voice shook and squeaked slightly–but they seemed to be determined to say their piece.

"Whatever. People like that deserve what they get.

Those people don't get an easy life any more than we do."
The second voice was harsh, sounding almost pleased.

"Moth, come on. They didn't do anything to you."
The first voice still sounded nervous but was more forceful
now, and Theo hissed in recognition.

"Shut up, Q," Moth said. "I'm tired of listening to
your bitching tonight. Sit down and have a beer."

"Moth, people were *hurt* today. And you still don't
know what all those symbols mean. Someone could get
killed!"

"Good! The world could use less of those assholes,"
Moth said smugly. "And that's what I'm figuring out, isn't
it? I may not be nerd-smart like you but I can see. I can
work out which symbol did what. I like that shitty traffic
one. Makes people walk more, and I can snag 'em into an
alley when they're not paying attention. Assholes like that
never pay attention and always seem to have cash." Moth
barked out a laugh, and Theo realized that this must be the
mugger, on top of everything.

Ivette's words from earlier flashed through his mind.
She had very clearly referred to the vandal's scribblings as
"glyphs", was that what these two were discussing? But
how could some paint end up hurting anyone? Theo's
mind provided the answer but he refused to entertain it.
There's no way. He frowned as he glanced around as if
there were answers written on the trees. Just as he was
about to laugh at that thought his eyes fell on a symbol,
spray painted heavily enough on the trunk of a tree that
drips of paint hung off the lines. Ice shot up his spine.

"Moth–" Quinn's protest was cut off by a sharp slap.
There was a soft thud and the younger voice grunted.
Theo didn't even think before he burst off the trail,
tingles prickling across his skin. Just past the trees–barely
even hidden from view, in fact–was a small clearing with

a shed and two young men: Quinn on the ground, clearly surprised, and the older one, Moth, sneering over him.

The taller, beefier man–Moth–looked even less pleasant than he had the other morning from across the river, smudges of dirt dotting his baggy jeans. Quinn glared up at his companion, his blonde hair a mess and his loose jacket sporting a few new smudges now as well, from where he had landed in the weedy dust. Neither of them even glanced at him, too deep in their argument to notice his abrupt arrival.

"Backhanding me isn't going to change the facts, Moth," Quinn said with a glare. "Innocent people are getting hurt because you're pissed off and feeling invincible. You shouldn't have stolen that book in the first place, but whatever. And if you were just going after that harpy, I'd get that, even if I didn't like it. But you're just randomly attacking people! That's not okay. That's not what I agreed to."

"You *agreed* to do what I told you, that's what you agreed to," Moth sneered.

"Hey!" Theo had no idea where the idea to interrupt came from, but it absolutely didn't originate in his rational, conscious mind. He tried not to shake as two pairs of shocked eyes turned to him. "Hey, whatever is going on here, I think I've heard enough to call the cops with. Besides the assault I just witnessed, it's pretty clear you're the vandal everyone's been looking for."

"How the *hell* did you find your way back here?" Moth snarled.

Theo blinked at him, slowly. "Um, I followed the shouting. It wasn't exactly difficult, the hiking trail is right there."

"Those glyphs shoulda kept you out. You shouldn'ta

heard us at all." Moth frowned, and Quinn scrambled to his feet.

"Maybe they wore out." Theo thought about the symbol in the tree. "Maybe a woodpecker put a hole in one of them. Maybe you didn't copy them right, who knows and who cares? The point is you're done."

"It's over, Moth!" Quinn said, drawing their attention.

"Like hell it's over," Moth snarled again. His eyes blazed with fury and Theo's heart lurched in his chest. There was something very wrong with the man. "I'm not stopping just cause of one asshole finding our camp."

Moth spun on his booted foot and charged at Theo, who stood there, shocked.

Everything slowed down. Theo had never once been in a physical confrontation, and he had no idea what to do. He could see Moth almost flying at him, his arm coming up to throw a punch with his full weight behind it. The victorious sneer on his face told Theo everything he needed to know about how comfortable the other man was with inflicting violence, and it occurred to him that the only way that Theo wouldn't be talking to anyone about this exchange was if he was dead.

He wondered if they'd throw his body in the river to be found by some passing student. Or Marielle. That would be entertaining, maybe. She would, no doubt, be deeply offended by the idea of a dead body anywhere near her self-appointed domain. He doubted she would miss him, though.

Just as the heavy fist was about to land, a blinding flash of light exploded from somewhere near Theo's chest. A wave of warmth and security washed over Theo and he took a gulp of air, realizing now that he had been holding his breath as he braced for the blow. Moth, however, flew backward like he had been caught in an explosion, landed near the shed, and rolled into one of the flimsy walls making the whole structure lurch alarmingly.

"Holy shit," Quinn whispered into the silence that fell immediately after the light died. Theo blinked at him. He was as shocked as the young man looked.

"Where the *hell* would an asshole like you get a charm like that? Find it in that haunted house the old man died in?" Moth grumbled.

"Doesn't much matter to you where I got it, does it?" Theo decided that brazen bullshit was probably his best bet here.

"It's over Moth. You can't beat him up and he's going to go to the cops for sure, now. Give up." Quinn stepped between Theo and the thug who was getting to his feet. "Come on, it's not worth it."

Moth growled. "You on *their* side now, Q? After everything I've done for you? I thought you were on my side. I thought you knew that they're not worth shit."

"I never signed up for random violence and aimless aggression, Moth. I wanted a place to be. People who didn't care what I wanted to do and wouldn't throw me out because it didn't fit their narrow worldview. I never agreed to join a gang or whatever it is you think you're doing here." Quinn gestured around the clearing and Theo noticed the empty beer cans and food wrappers. "I sure as hell never signed up to be your personal servant and housekeeper."

"You're not with me, then you're as bad as they are, and you're going to go down with 'em." Moth snarled. He reached behind himself with one hand to pull out a gun and with his left hand he reached up over his shaved head to grab... air as far as Theo could tell. But as soon as he closed his hand, the air in the thug's hand glowed.

"I been reading that damn book, Q. You think I don't

know what those glyphs are for? You think I'm too stupid to understand what's written down in there?"

"Moth, what are you doing?"

Quinn trembled and his voice shook. Theo reached out and pulled him back behind him, hoping that whatever Avery's gift had done to prevent the beating would also work against whatever it was Moth was doing now.

Well, the gun he understood at least, but whatever the *hell* was going on in the man's left hand was straight out of some sort of crazy nightmare. The light was pulsing and turning a sickly yellow-green.

"Now, which way should I do this? I don't think the book is really all that good. None of the glyphs did *exactly* what the book said they would, so I dunno if this will melt a hole in you or not. But I've got my backup here in case, so either way." Moth laughed as he waved his gun, but it sounded wrong to Theo's ears.

"Don't try anything, Moth. I have no idea what this charm will do. It blew you back ten feet for just trying to punch me, I'm pretty sure trying to melt me would provoke a stronger reaction." Theo honestly worried that they might somehow blow a hole in the forest. It didn't make any sense, but then sense and logic had long since left the clearing.

"Hah!" Moth actually said the word, scorn dripping from the syllable. "You have no idea, do you? You live in that nutjob's house and you have no *clue*! Haven't you read any of those moldy old books? That thing's dead, you idiot. It used its juice. It can't save you now. You're both dead."

He brought his left hand down and held his fist of nauseating light near his shoulder, then shoved it forward and opened his fingers. The light started to move, like the slow toss of a ball in a kid's dodgeball game. Theo had never been any good at dodgeball.

"Shit!" Quinn shoved Theo sideways, making him stumble and hit the ground just as someone barreled into the clearing from behind them and met the glowing light head-on with a clear, iridescent light of his own.

"Well. I guess we get to have show-and-tell today after all," Avery said with a smirk in his voice.

19

NOT SO SECRET ANYMORE

Theo blinked up at his new friend for a moment before Quinn reached down to help him back to his feet. The young man stood slightly behind Theo and stared, wide-eyed at Avery, and honestly, Theo didn't blame him. Now he understood why the man had been taking off his shirt earlier.

Avery stood there in his usual jeans and biker boots but no shirt, his aqua hair a mess and his piercings twinkling in the faint glow coming off his wings.

Avery had goddamned fairy wings.

"What... what the hell?" Theo's rational mind left the clearing to join his sense and reason. All three were probably trying to find a bar that didn't have a big hole in the front because this evening definitely required alcohol to start making any sense.

"You're a fucking *fairy?*" Moth shouted. "What the fuck?"

Avery sighed. "No, as a matter of fact. I'm a pixie, but I'm also not going to waste my breath explaining all the differences. You're standing there wielding a gun and magic you have no idea how to control. And, if I am putting the pieces together correctly, you're the one responsible for all the mayhem in the area lately. My boss is pissed about his bar, and I heard about the Cardosos. And now you're threatening my friend Theo? Nope."

His wings fluttered slightly, leaving the faintest of rainbows in their wake, before they flapped hard and sort of folded in on themselves, disappearing into Avery's back.

"That's a neat trick," Theo muttered.

"Yeah. Handy for, you know, wearing shirts." Avery answered, but didn't take his eyes off Moth.

"I am not going to lose to a fucking *fairy*."

"See, now I can't tell if you're being slow on the uptake or deliberately offensive." Avery stepped forward like having a gun pointed at him was not a concern. "Not that there's anything particularly wrong with fairies. I mean, okay, yes. Fairies do tend toward the more delicate end of the spectrum, but they're tough. Like roses. Delicate and pretty and more than happy to stab you if you try to get rough."

He took another step forward. "You think you're tough enough to take me out? I promise you that sad magic isn't going to help you, and that gun is both boring and cheap. Do you have a *real* weapon on you? A knife or something?"

"You think a bitch with glitter wings can beat me? I don't fucking need this for you. Sure will make it faster though."

Moth swung the gun toward Avery at the same time as Avery exploded into motion. He had been creeping closer to the man the whole time they were talking and Moth hadn't been paying enough attention. Avery flowed. It was the only word Theo could come up with to describe what happened. Within seconds the gun was flying harmlessly across the clearing to skitter into a pile of leaves and Moth himself was on the ground, face down in the dust.

"Do we have any rope or... something?" Avery looked up at Theo and Quinn, his eyes sparkling in the light from the fire pit. "I mean, I suppose I could hold him here until the police show up, but…"

"I have so many questions," Theo said.

Me too," Quinn croaked.

Avery grinned. "I bet. I can probably guess a few of them. Let's see. No, you're not hallucinating. Yes, magic very much exists, and if you recall I did try to tell you that this morning, Theo. I knew you were in trouble because my buddy put a little tag in that charm that alerted me when the charm expended itself, and I just followed the sudden flare of magic here. I was surprised that the charm blew that hot, but once I got here I realized it was reacting to this jerk's ham-fisted spellcasting."

Theo blinked.

"Um, are you going to..." Quinn's nervous voice petered out.

Avery's gaze shifted and his eyebrow quirked up, making the eyebrow ring wink. "We're going to get the police out here and get this jerk arrested for all sorts of things, not least of which being assault, and attempted murder. And probably vandalism, if I'm guessing right."

"You are," Quinn said.

"We're going to have to come up with something to tell the cops, though. 'My buddy's magic charm let me know he needed help so I flew to the scene to stop an angry jerk from using magic he didn't understand' isn't really going to go down well in the police reports," Avery said, scrunching up his face to punctuate his thought. Moth's struggles under his hands didn't seem to disturb Avery in the slightest. "And my shirt fell out of my back pocket somewhere back in the trees."

"Um, how about we say that you and I were out for a hike? I... um. I have no idea what to say about your shirt, though," Theo said.

"Oh! You can borrow one of mine. It'll be a little small on you, but I think it'll be okay," Quinn said. "I'm Quinn Lawson, by the way. Thanks for saving us."

"Avery Steele. It was no trouble at all. And I'll take the shirt, sure."

Quinn nodded and disappeared into the shed. Theo met Avery's gaze and held it for a long moment, the sounds of the forest and the snap of a log in the fire pit the only noise they heard aside from Moth's snarling.

"You're going to have a lot of talking to do, you realize that, right?" Theo said at last.

"I figured," Avery said with a grin. "Welcome to the rabbit hole, Alice."

Quinn came out with a sheet he ripped into strips to tie Moth's wrists and a T-shirt that was probably baggy on him but fit Avery like a second skin. Theo watched Avery's muscles moved under the skin of his back and shoulder, and marveled that there was absolutely no hint of the wings that they had all seen clear as day, that Avery had *flown into the clearing with*.

Magic. Holy shit.

The police showed up in short order once Theo called them. Quinn pressed close to his side, seeking comfort as much as possible until they were separated to give their statements. The cops hauled Moth–whose real name turned out to be Mark Amstead–off to the back of a patrol car and returned with Detective Angelo, who demanded to know what the hell was going on.

According to Quinn, Moth had lost his parents young

and been raised by his aunt—one Marielle Trevor—who kicked him to the curb when he turned eighteen and she and her husband moved to Greenwoods.

When they *finally* got back to his house, hours later, Theo let them in the back door right into the kitchen.

"So, basically he was pissed at his aunt for… well, let's be honest. He was just angry. I can't even blame him for that," Theo said. He was making coffee and Avery sat, once again shirtless at Theo's kitchen table. Quinn sat across from him, eyes still wide and wary, watching both of them.

"She's pretty awful. I was actually out there hiding from her tonight. She came pounding on my door and screeching so I snuck out the back," Theo admitted.

He flipped the switch on his coffeepot and turned to lean a hip on the counter. Leonidas sauntered in and blinked at Avery who smiled back at the creature. The cat turned to Quinn for a moment before brushing against Theo's legs as if to reassure them both that Theo was fine. Then Leo stepped delicately over to the table and leaped up to settle in the startled boy's lap as if he owned it, and purring loud enough that they could all hear it.

"So, how did Moth get that book?" Avery asked.

"We broke in here one night when it was pouring rain. Mr. McCann was dead and the place was empty so we figured nobody would care if we got out of the storm. That shed isn't the most waterproof place ever," Quinn said quietly. "We dried off in here and were going to just hang out, but the place was so *weird*…" Quinn shot a glance at Theo and ducked his head. "Sorry."

"No worries. I thought the same thing when I moved in. Gruncle Garfield seems to have collected everything he touched," Theo said with a shrug.

"Anyway, I wandered around a bit once I stopped dripping and got totally lost in some of the books I found. God, I'd never seen so many books outside of a library!" Quinn's eyes shone with excitement, and he sat up straight.

"Well, that sounds like a kindred soul," a new voice commented from the hallway. "Shirt delivery, Ave. Here you go." The newcomer stepped into the kitchen and held out a black shirt. "I'm sorry for just barging in. The front door was unlocked and I guessed you'd want this fool covered. And I'm kind of used to just wandering in when I wanted to borrow a book or something, sorry. I'm Darren Langston, Avery's cousin and housemate."

The newcomer was as tall as Avery, but slim and wiry where Avery was muscular. He had bright blonde hair swept off his forehead and the most aggressively nerdy glasses Theo had ever seen to go with his sunset-colored bowtie and sky blue cardigan. Darren and Avery looked almost nothing at all alike.

"It's no problem. Theobold Warren. Call me Theo." Theo shook the hand offered to him. "And that's Quinn Lawson. Coffee?"

"God, please." Darren sank into a chair next to Quinn and the cat allowed him to scratch behind his ears for a moment.

"You're Avery's cousin?" Quinn peered at the slim man. "Are you..."

Darren laughed. "Yes, I am also a pixie, though I'm no warrior. I'm a scholar. I work up at the college in the history department."

"What–"

"No skipping around!" Theo cut Quinn off before they could go too far down the rabbit hole of questions. Lord knew there were enough questions to last them days, and Theo's near miss with getting arrested for vandalism earlier in the day, not to mention nearly being killed in the woods by a rejected nephew was currently taking priority right this second. "Tell us about the book."

"Ooh, a book story!" Darren propped his head on his fist and turned to Quinn. "What book?"

"Um, I..."

Quinn frowned and took a moment to get his thoughts back together. Theo took the opportunity to grab mugs and the milk from the fridge, then handed them around. The coffee finished, and as Theo sat back down at the table with it Quinn picked his story back up.

"Right. So. I was looking at all the books in the other room, and Moth came up and snatched one away from me, kind of mocking me a bit. Reading pages at random out loud like he was making fun of the subject, but the more he did it, the less he read out loud. I didn't really pay much attention, cause I was looking at other books. It was... I mean..."

"I get it. Like you don't even know where to start with how excited you are." Darren grinned. "Definitely some scholar in you."

"Huh?" Quinn blinked at Darren who waved it off.

"Later. Theo wants us to stay on track."

"So, I take it that Moth found the book with the glyphs in it here and took it with him when you went back to that shack in the woods?" Avery asked. He nodded his thanks for the coffee and added a bit of sugar before taking a drink.

Quinn nodded. "I didn't know he'd taken it till a few weeks later. I found it when I was collecting empty beer cans and stuff. Moth played it off like he was just using it for inspiration. That's about when he started buying spray paint and tagging things."

"And when he realized that the glyphs actually did

what the book said they'd do, he started to study," Avery said with a nod. "I can see that. A young punk thinks he's found something that gives him some power, gives him an edge, and suddenly thinks that he's invulnerable."

"God, what a sadly common story," Darren agreed with a grimace. "This coffee is perfect, Theo, thanks."

"Yeah, I guess that's what happened. He was pissed at his aunt for throwing him out and wanted revenge on her and all the people here who he said sneered at him for being young and poor," Quinn said. He stared down at his thumb on the mug handle. "He somehow decided that his aunt's stuff should belong to him, and there was something about life insurance from his parents and I don't really know. He only talked about it when he was super drunk and it didn't make much sense. I do know that he wanted to get back in here and find some more books about magic, but then Theo moved in and just about never left the house."

"Which is why he started doing more tagging around here in the neighborhood, which is why Marielle decided that I was responsible for it. In a way I sort of was, I just didn't do any of it."

They all sat with their thoughts on Moth and his revenge, and how it had affected everyone, until after several minutes Quinn reached for the carafe and refilled his coffee cup.

"So, who wants to start explaining the pixie thing?" he asked.

20

PIXIES AND NERDS

"Garfield seriously didn't explain anything before he died?" Darren looked genuinely startled. "I mean, he always told me that his nephew would fit into Greenwoods perfectly, that he was absolutely confident in you."

It was Theo's turn to be startled. "I was barely aware of the man. I only met him once when I was a kid, so when the lawyer called to tell me about the will I was shocked. Confident about what?"

"Really?" Darren screwed his face up in a thoughtful frown. "That's so odd. He knew all about you. We both enjoyed reading your articles, you're quite talented. I especially love your pieces on the dig in Saqqara, you really seem to enjoy the subject and it comes through in your work."

"I do." Theo frowned in return. "Thanks? What does that have to do with Garfield?"

"Well, you told me a bit about your mom. Maybe Garfield was hesitant to get in touch with you because he realized her animosity and guessed that she would block communications?" Avery suggested.

"I'm thirty-one years old. I'm pretty certain that my mother has no control over my cell phone any longer," he said dryly.

"Well, at any rate, Garfield should have told you," Darren said. "There has been a member of your family here for, oh, at least nine generations. The earliest record we have found so far for your family here is 1804, but they reference family that had been established for some time already. I suspect that if we had written records we could trace your lineage back through the native people of the area, at least in your direct line."

Theo blinked at him. "What?"

"I can show you the records Garfield had. Some of those old journals are fascinating." Darren's eyes lit up and he leaned forward but Avery caught him by the shoulder and chuckled.

"Later, cuz. Right now we've got some explaining to do, remember?" he said.

"That's amazing, though," Quinn said. "It must be nice to know about your family. My mom died when I was a baby and my dad never talked about her. He wasn't close to his own family either, but they're from all over as far as I can tell. They were all jerks though, so no loss there, but your uncle sounds like he was cool."

"I wouldn't know," Theo said faintly.

"So, Warren family tree aside, I am, as I think I mentioned, a pixie. So's Darren." Avery turned to eye Quinn. "And maybe you? What did your dad tell you?"

"He wasn't the best dad ever by a long shot, but he would have mentioned something like that, I'm pretty sure. I think... You, um... you had wings back there, but you don't now." Quinn gripped his mug in both hands.

"Yeah." Avery pulled off his shirt again and turned in his chair to show his back. It was smooth and muscular but otherwise looked simply like the back of someone in excellent shape. Until there was a ripple, like heat pouring off the pavement in the summer, then wings unfurled from his back and fluttered delicately, shimmering in the light of the kitchen.

"Holy shit," Theo muttered. They were shaped like butterfly wings, broad and rounded at the corners but dipping down a bit at the bottom to come to a slightly ragged point. But rather than being bright and flashy, they were clear and iridescent like dragonfly wings, the vein structure–Theo had no real idea about wings, but he thought the lines that shot through the filmy membrane must be veins–were a deep, glittery blue near Avery's back and lighter, almost white-blue near the edges. A faint stirring of the air brushed against his skin as they fanned slowly back and forth.

"Holy crap! How… What?" Quinn was pushed back in his chair, staring with his mouth gaping before lunging closer to peer at them. "Do they work? I mean, can you fly?"

"You *saw* me fly into the clearing," Avery pointed out.

"So, pixies, fairies, and elves all come from the same realm, the same dimension if you will," Darren said.

Theo only listened with half an ear while he gaped at the display in front of him. Avery met his gaze and Theo thought he saw a flicker of nerves in his friend

"Fairies are real too? What's the difference? thought fairies and pixies were the same thing?" Quinn asked.

"We're similar in many regards, but no. It's a bit like saying wolves and coyotes are the same, though that's a pretty bad comparison. But no, pixies and fairies are not the same," Avery said.

He looked over his shoulder and caught Theo's eye again, an unspoken worry now firmly settled there. Theo could only blink back, unsure of anything now that the very foundations of his life had been shaken.

"How..." That was not a very intelligent question. Hell, it was barely a fully formed thought, but Darren seemed to understand.

"Once upon a time—" Darren started.

"Hah! Don't all fairy tales start that way?" Quinn asked, smirking.

"Anyway, once upon a time, way before I can find any records, this realm had waypoints. They—"

"Waypoints?" Theo interrupted and Darren gave him a withering glance.

"Yes," he answered despite the irritation. "Waypoints. Portals. Places where the veil is thin between worlds, if you're feeling poetic and a little new-agey. Whatever you like to call them. This world had a number of them scattered around the planet, and since it was a neutral space, a place where all magics seemed to work well enough, the people from those other worlds came through the waypoints to trade or visit or, well, do all the things that people generally want to travel to do." Darren shrugged. "Once upon a time, for many people, traveling between the realms was no more of a hassle than travel between countries, and just like international travel, there were only certain places you could do it."

"These waypoints," Quinn murmured. "They were like border crossing checkpoints."

"More like ports, but I think you get it," Avery said. He had sat back down in his seat and picked up his coffee, but his wings still shimmered softly. Theo was having a hard time reconciling the "pixie" and the "punk bouncer" aspects of it all. Avery's eyebrow piercing seemed to wink at him, and when he glanced up, Avery was grinning at him. "And just like any border crossing, there were border guards. There are no records of the beginnings of all this, mind you, and I'm the wrong one of us to ask about it, but from what I understand it is generally believed that while the waypoint guardians were originally gifted humans–"

"Priests, shamans, that sort of thing," Darren jumped in. "It is a commonly accepted theory that while these guards started out as simply human, they interbred very early on with those who traveled through the waypoints and their children gained some of the abilities and skills."

"The border guards got it on with the travelers because that's what you do in a port town, is that the basic gist of it?" Theo had to smirk at the image that sprang into his mind of an ancient priest stripping off his ceremonial headdress at a tavern and ordering a beer while complaining to the bartender about passports and customs forms.

Quinn snickered and Avery grinned wider, but Darren just nodded. "Essentially, yes. The guardian families got a bit stronger, and years passed with the usual immigration and trade and so on and then after centuries, the waypoints started closing. Just stopped working for reasons we are still researching today. The waypoint here closed just over a century and a half ago and has only reopened once for three hours since then. The Cardoso family started from the dryads that stumbled through seeking sanctuary."

Theo sat up and blinked at Darren. "The Cardosos? Stacy and Jorge and the boys?"

Darren nodded and Avery added, "And your neighbor Ivette, though her mom married into a line of witches, so she's kind of special. And Artie's friend Holly and her mom are dryads as well. And I think you met Mateo? His family are shifters. There's lots of different non-human families around in Whitelake, and especially in Greenwoods."

"Wow, okay." Theo sat back in his chair and even though he knew it was rude, kept staring at Avery's wings.

"Anyway, none of that is especially important except that it means that there are more than humans living here now, because people got trapped on this side when the waypoints shut down and became so erratic," Avery said with a shrug. "It was not great, but like any people who get stuck, those who were trapped here made the best of it. It's not a bad place to live, after all. Our people lived and thrived and married and had kids and *they* lived and had kids and so on. And now here we are. At this point, people like Darren and I are as much from this realm as you are, really. Neither of us has ever been to the Fae realm, and I'm pretty sure I wouldn't want to go. I'm fine here."

Darren nodded and Quinn frowned into his coffee cup for a long moment. He swallowed heavily and Theo couldn't help seeing the pain in his eyes when he looked up at Darren.

"My mom was a pixie, wasn't she? That's what you meant earlier."

Darren smiled softly and nodded. "I think so, yes. You have a fair amount of magic in you. I bet if you closed your eyes and really thought about it you could sense ours. I would guess that you're a scholar, like I am."

Quinn blinked hard and a crease formed between his brows. "What do you mean? I never even finished high school."

Darren gasped. "How... what?"

"I was kinda homeless, and it got too hard to keep up with my classes and stay safe once I ran out of friends' sofas to sleep on. Their parents always wanted to call my dad, and..." Quinn shrugged.

"Wow. Okay." Darren ran his fingers through his short hair, making it stand on end. "Okay, well the short explanation is that pixies, and to a lesser extent fairies and elves, tend to fall into one of three predispositions: scholars, warriors, and crafters. It's not like a casual interest sort of thing, either. It's like an innate drive. The traits usually run in families, but not always. My dad was the only scholar in his family."

Theo leaned forward and looked at Avery. "And you're a warrior."

"Yep!" Avery answered with a grin. "My uncle was sort of the black sheep of his family. Went off and married another scholar, and here we are."

Quinn gasped and sat up straight in his chair. "That's why Dad kept trying to make me take those martial arts classes! Theo, do you think he knew?"

"I couldn't say," he answered honestly. "I wonder about your mother, though."

"It would explain so much, though!" Quinn said before slumping down again. "Not that it matters. If he did know, why wouldn't he tell me? And if it's not a guarantee what a kid turns out to be, why did he force me to go to all those classes? And what do I do now?"

Darren reached out and took Quinn's hand. "First step, you get your GED. You'll feel much more settled with some educational credentials to your name, I can tell you that. And after that we'll figure it out from there."

"So what does this all mean?" Theo said before yawning so widely his jaw clicked. "Ugh, sorry."

"It's late, and today has felt like it lasted weeks. Don't be sorry," Avery said, looking at his phone. "I mean, I'm usually in bed by now and I work at a bar. I vote we all get some rest and figure out everything else tomorrow. Quinn, where are you living?"

Quinn bit his lip and wouldn't meet Theo's eyes. "I slept in Moth's shack mostly."

Theo blinked. "And you've been sleeping in my shed sometimes too, haven't you? That's your box of camping supplies, not Gruncle Garfield's." God, half of the weird stuff he'd noticed over the last few weeks was making a hell of a lot more sense.

Quinn turned pink, as if he had a fast-forwarded sunburn. "I'm sorry. I'll clear it all out and find somewhere else to stay."

Darren frowned. "Where?"

"Not sure." Quinn shrugged "I'll figure it out."

"I'd offer you space at our house, but we're seriously out of room. Darren turned the living room and the breakfast nook into libraries, and there were only two bedrooms to start with. You could probably stay here," Avery said, glancing around the kitchen thoughtfully. "I'd bet there's a bunch of empty rooms upstairs."

"And it's less full of garden supplies," Darren added before frowning at the door to the cluttered living room. "Maybe."

"Um, it's not your house, guys," Quinn pointed out.

Theo sighed, mentally. "No, it's mine. And they're right. There's plenty of room for you here, at least until you get yourself figured out. But there still might be gardening supplies, Darren's right. The old man was a packrat of the first order."

The three men started talking about what Quinn needed, beyond bringing his books in from Theo's shed, where he had apparently been keeping them safe from Moth. Plans were made to get him some new clothes for his job at the Last Pot, and Darren started plotting out how to get Quinn's pixie half settled with his studies.

The cat purred loud enough that it was a soft, rumbling undertone to the whole conversation.

So much for his quiet, stress-free life. Allowing Quinn to stay here seemed like it was going to be both very social and slightly chaotic for a while. Theo realized he wasn't mad about it at all.

21

FAMILY

Theo groaned and woke up enough to swear as he rolled over to reach for his phone. He had finally gotten Quinn settled and the cousins out by four in the morning and he had looked forward with incredible satisfaction to sleeping in for half the day. It was not to be, it seemed, and he swore silently as his fingers finally reached their target.

"'lo?" he grunted into the phone.

"Theobold? Are you still asleep? Did I call too early again?" His mother's voice rang through the phone and he tried not to groan.

He peered at his clock and worked out that it said nine fourteen.

"No, Mom, but we were up very late last night and I was looking forward to not having to wake until lunch."

"Well it's eleven o'clock here, so that's reasonably close to lunchtime, I think. What on earth were you doing to stay up so late? You're usually more responsible than that."

Without pausing she launched into a recitation of what she and his father were doing–he was thinking of retiring, but probably wouldn't for another few years, which came up often enough that Theo didn't even bother replying—and about the Girls In Science mentoring program she volunteered for, and so on. She rambled on and he scratched his head and then down his chest and yawned before sitting up while he listened to his mother's gossip routine. She went through it at least once a week with him before she worked her way to the purpose of her call. He might as well get up and make himself some coffee—this was likely to take a while.

He shuffled into the kitchen to the most glorious sight: Quinn turning around with a full pot of coffee, an empty cup, and an understanding tilt to his eyebrows. He waved Theo to the table and put the cup down in front of him before filling it up to the brim with the fuel that would make this call bearable. Theo mouthed the words "bless you," before lifting the cup and taking his first sip of life-giving fuel. Quinn just chuckled and went back to the counter.

"So, that's what's going on with us. Oh, that nice pizza place you loved is closing. I guess the owners are trying to sell instead of just shut down, but it's not looking good for some reason."

Theo blinked. "Bently's? Why? That place is always busy."

He could imagine his mother's shrug. "No idea. I chatted with the fellow who made our pizza the other day, and he growled about the man who owns the place—the business guy not the manager—not knowing a damn thing about good customer relations or keeping his fingers off the books. I guess the owner had a partner or something who left and now he's not doing so well. Sounds like his old partner was a better businessman."

Theo frowned at the half a cup he had left before swallowing it all down at once. That didn't make a damn bit of sense. Unless they hired a new manager for the place, Jerry and Penny didn't even have to touch Bently's to make money from it. In fact, probably shouldn't touch it.

Theo needed more coffee for this.

"I don't know what to tell you, Mom," Theo said, though he was already planning to call their–Jerry's– manager when he was more fully awake. He had always had a good relationship with their ground-level people, soothing ruffled feathers and making the real decisions while Jerry was the face of the corporation and dealt with all the board meetings and so on.

Quinn grinned again as he refilled Theo's cup and then fussed around at the stove. Soon the smell of frying bacon wafted through the air, and Theo made a note to tell Quinn his rent could be paid in coffee and bacon if he decided to just stay. It was surprisingly nice to have someone else in this house in the morning. Felt less... hollow, somehow.

His mother rattled on for a few more minutes before asking, finally, "So what could possibly keep you up so late?"

"Oh, remember I mentioned that there's been a rash of vandalism around here? Well, I accidentally stumbled onto the vandal's hideout last night. The police kept us all out for a while getting stories and statements and so on, and then we came back here to wind down from that mess after."

Quinn put a plate in front of him then took the seat he'd occupied the night before. Theo gazed at the breakfast bounty, then murmured another quick "thanks" to the young man who was being a damn godsend this morning.

"Is someone there?" his mother cut into her old refrain of "just sell the house and come home."

"Um, yeah. A young man named Quinn. He's staying here for a while and is possibly an actual saint. He made coffee *and* breakfast." Theo dug in with gusto knowing that his mother would be talking for a while. He wasn't wrong, and by the time she wound down he had heard all about the dangers of trusting strangers in your home, how to be a good roommate, and of course, cleaning out the house and using it as a rental property when he came home.

"Mom, I'm not moving back to Nebraska," Theo cut into her monologue when she stopped to take a breath. "I know you don't like that I'm so far away, but I have to live my own life, and right now, that life is here."

There was a moment of silence before she sighed. "Why, though, Theo? What is there for you all the way in Oregon that you can't find here?"

Theo pushed his plate away and leaned back in his chair. Quinn raised an eyebrow at him then turned back to the book he had out which looked like one of Garfield's weird history books in German. Wait, Quinn could read German?

"Well, it's maybe not that Whitelake has specific, tangible things that Omaha lacks, I think," Theo answered slowly. He scrubbed his hand over his head and the thought drifted through his mind that he needed a haircut soon. "I think it's just a fresh start. New place, new chance to discover what makes me happy, you know?"

"But sweetheart, you're thirty-one years old. You already know what makes you happy."

"Do I? I thought I did, certainly. But now that I can look back at my life with Penny, I realize that I was mostly doing what made *her* happy. And that's not the same thing."

Quinn scraped the last bite from his plate then collected the dishes and took them to the sink. Theo smiled his thanks and kept speaking. "I'm making friends here, Mom. I found a great cafe and a good bar. The college isn't too far away and they often need temps so when I get stir crazy writing at home I can find something to do. Most of my neighbors are nice, and the house is definitely growing on me. And I need you to stop pressuring me to move back, okay?"

There was a long, heavy silence from the other end of the phone. "Is there something you're not telling me? Are you n some kind of trouble?"

Theo glanced at Quinn, who had sat down again and was deeply engrossed in the book. *There's a hell of a lot that I'm not telling you.*

"Mom. I don't have to be in trouble or keeping secrets to want to live my own life." He tried another tactic. "Your parents didn't approve of you going to college for science, right? They didn't want you to be a chemist instead of a teacher or a nurse before becoming a housewife, but you knew what was right for you, and you did it anyway and found happiness and success, right? This is the same thing. You don't want me to live so far away, which I can understand, but I need to do what's right for me. Okay?"

She sighed, the sound resigned. "Okay, sweetheart. But I do miss you."

"I know, Mom. I miss you too. That's why we have phones and video chats and vacation visits and all that, right?" Theo smirked and rolled his eyes, safe in knowing that she couldn't see him. This wasn't a video chat, after all.

After a few more minutes, his mother hung up the phone and Theo slumped back in his chair.

"She sounds... nice, mostly," Quinn commented after a moment. He glanced up from his book and raised his eyebrow at Theo.

"Thank you for breakfast, before I forget to say something. But yes. She is, mostly. Surprisingly supportive with most of my life. Like I told Avery, though, she's very science-minded. She didn't like Great-uncle Garfield much at all, since he was very..." Theo blinked, feeling some pieces slip into place. "Holy shit. He knew."

"He knew?" Quinn frowned. "Knew what?"

"Gruncle Garfield knew about magic. About... about all this stuff," Theo glared around the kitchen as if he was half expecting something magical to jump out at him. "Darren said he's used to just wandering in and borrowing books. All the weird books about mythology and the occult that I've been finding everywhere? That's why he knew all those magic tricks and kept talking about mythology and fairy tales when we were here. I was a kid, I never thought anything about it. Mom *hated* it, though. Started to take me out all day and go hiking or to the museum up at the college. We were supposed to be here for a week, but we only stayed for the long weekend before we headed out to the cabin they had rented for the week at Lake Wenatchee."

"He knew your mom didn't like him?" Quinn asked.

Theo chuckled. "She isn't one for being subtle. She made very clear her opinions of his 'immature hobbies' and 'infantile fascination with fantasy,' and for the knockout blow she went on about encouraging a child to remain blind to reality and how it would take possibly years to undo the damage he wreaked upon my fragile psyche." Theo sent Quinn a bland glance. "I was eight."

Quinn stayed quiet for a moment. "Well, maybe he saw something in you back then that seemed like you would fit here? Do you have any cousins? Er, cousins once removed? Second cousins? Whatever they're called, I have no idea about family relationships and genealogy." Quinn scrunched up his face.

"Probably?" Theo shrugged. "I have no real idea. My mom didn't like Great-uncle Garfield and my grandparents passed away when I was really young. Dad was an only child. If there's any other family on that side I've never met them. And we weren't close to Mom's family."

"Yeah, I didn't mean to eavesdrop, but you did mention it on the phone," Quinn said.

"I know she had siblings, but I only met my aunts a couple of times. I'd be surprised if they didn't have kids. And of course, I'm not sure if Garfield had more siblings himself, other than my grandfather."

"Maybe you should look into it? I dunno. There must be some reason." Quinn tipped his head to the side. "You do seem like you're in the right place, though. I can't really explain it. It's just... You feel *right* here. It was even more noticeable last night by Moth's shed." Quinn shook his head before continuing, his voice more hesitant. "I used to sleep in your garden shed when Moth was being especially violent and drunk. I just felt safer there. Last night, climbing into that bed in the guest room was the safest I've ever felt, even before I had the fight with my dad. The house didn't feel like that when we came to get out of the storm. I think all that is related to you."

A warm feeling sparked to life in Theo's chest. "Related to me?"

Quinn nodded and peered at Theo thoughtfully. "I think so. There's something..." Quinn pursed his lips and a crease formed between his brows. "There's something about you that's... I'm not sure I can really describe it. Safe, in a way, but..." He let out a frustrated grunt after a few moments of struggling. "Remember when we met at the Last Pot?"

"I do. I'm glad you got the job, by the way. Congratulations."

"Thanks." Quinn smiled quietly for a moment. "But yeah. I don't normally tell my life story to someone I basically just met. I mean sure, I knew who you were, and we had that chat by the river that once, and I was sleeping next to your lawnmower more often than not lately, but still. And somehow I knew that your garden shed, in particular, would be a safe place for me to hide when Moth was on one of his benders. It was just a knowing, deep in my bones. Like when you walk into some churches or temples and you just *know* not to swear or be rude."

Theo let that sit for a few minutes and wondered if maybe there was something to what Quinn was trying to say. Gruncle Garfield didn't leave any letters or instructions or anything when he died. Just his will and his very detailed instructions on who to pass the estate down to.

"Maybe your cousins are jerks." Quinn shrugged. "Either way, I'm glad you did get the house. I'm glad I met you."

Theo felt his ears getting hot, but so was the little spark in his chest. "I am too, actually."

Quinn grinned suddenly, looking for all the world like he knew he was about to get into trouble. "I always wondered what it would be like to have siblings, and by the time they left, Avery and Darren sorta felt like they adopted me. Now I've got a new dad, too! I mean, you're in your *thirties!* You're *old!*"

"Just for that little insult, you're grounded, kid," Theo grumbled, but he knew he was smiling too.

22

EPILOGUE

Quinn was settled into the living room with the book of history. Theo finally asked if he could read German, and Quinn said he could stumble through it a little, but never had any formal training or anything. He just picked up a couple of language books at the library because a lot of history was written in German and he loved history. Theo could only shake his head and be impressed. He had never managed to learn more than high school Spanish, himself, and even that was not what he'd call useful.

Being able to ask where the bathroom is will only help you if you can understand the answer, after all.

Theo was back in the little library room, continuing to clean and dust. It took three hours but the room was now mostly random-stuff-free. The small vial of swirling golden... Whatever-it-was sat on top of a pair of artistically stacked books on the small table by the chair and Theo huffed a small laugh at the thought that it had only been a day since Avery had tried to tell him that magic was real.

Well, he was a believer now.

The sound of the door opening shook him out of his thoughts and he picked up the box of who-knew-what-all and carried it out with him.

"Hey, what's all that?" Darren asked, plopping down on the sofa beside Quinn.

"Random magpie collection stuff Gruncle Garfield left in the library." Theo carried the box over to the hall and tucked it out of the way next to the door. He'd sort the sticks and pebbles out later. He had found some pretty neat coins in there, too, to add to one of his bowls. Maybe he ought to get them appraised...

Darren chuckled. "Yeah. He was definitely a packrat. Every time we went for a walk by the river or in the woods he'd come back with a pocket full of treasures like a kid."

Avery chuckled as he walked in from the kitchen, mugs of coffee in hand. He passed one to Darren and one to Quinn before turning to hand a third to Theo. "I hope you don't mind, I basically rummaged through your kitchen."

Theo shrugged. The truth was that he was remarkably okay with it. He'd never had friends that felt comfortable enough to just walk into his home and get things to drink. His life with Penny had been mainly working alone in his office, watching TV in the evenings with Penny when she was home, or meeting Penny's friends or Jerry out for drinks somewhere.

Before that, when he was still living at home with his parents, he was busy building his resume for college applications and studying. His parents both made sure he joined clubs and volunteered and got social interaction but rarely had anyone come over to just... hang out.

This? He watched Darren lean over and point at something in the book on Quinn's knees and Quinn bent over it, repeating the unfamiliar words while Avery watched, an amused grin on his face, and sipped his coffee. This was really nice, Theo decided.

He was about to sit down when the doorbell sounded. With a groan, he reversed course and headed for the hallway. When he opened the door he suppressed another groan.

"Good afternoon, Marielle, what can I do for you today?" he asked. The woman was the least pleasant thing about the neighborhood, and yet she was still a human being and deserved at least surface manners until further notice.

Marielle's lips flattened into a thin line. "I understand we have you to thank for the arrest of the vandal."

Theo stared at her for a moment, then glanced back over his shoulder where someone was laughing.

"Well, I stumbled across him, yes, but Avery is the one who disarmed him and held him until the police showed up." He felt a small fizz of satisfaction when she looked for a second like she had bitten into a lemon "Quinn helped as well, and he's going to be living here for a while. Safety in numbers and all that. Oh, and you'll be pleased to hear that I made a deal with Artie Cardoso to come mow my lawn every week. No more grass getting too tall. I was thinking of putting in a garden as well. Much more environmentally responsible than lawn, you know. I've written a few articles about it. I'd be happy to get my agent to send you copies of them if you like?"

Theo held back a smirk. When had he decided to kill her with kindness? It seemed to be working, at least.

A faint line formed between Marielle's brows and her lips got thinner, somehow. "I hardly think that a child is capable of the level of yard work required to keep up neighborhood appearances. And you will need to reference your HOA manual to find acceptable plantings. New plantings are strictly regulated for a uniform community standard." Her jaw was tight and Theo was a bit impressed that her hair didn't even move while she stood there, practically vibrating with her irritation.

He looked at her, then stepped onto the porch to turn and look up at the front of his house. It wasn't an elaborately gingerbreaded Victorian wonder, but it was still a beautiful example of the era. What it was not, most definitely, was new.

He turned back to her and thought that she would be at risk of a medical condition if she kept turning red like that.

"Marielle, I appreciate that you are trying to keep community standards at a certain level," Theo said. Maybe if he tried diplomacy she would get over herself for a few minutes. "But I think that a heavy-handed approach is only going to serve to alienate people and will not likely serve the neighborhood. Perhaps a lighter touch might work better?"

Marelle scoffed. "The only thing some people understand is blunt pronouncements. Apparently, you are one of those people. Follow the rules or there will be repercussions." And with that, she spun and stormed down the steps and to the sidewalk.

Theo sighed and took another sip of his coffee, which he realized he was still holding.

"Man, she needs a vacation or something," Avery said from just behind his shoulder. They both watched as she got into her SUV and slammed the door shut before driving off down the street.

"I think even the good Detective Angelo was over her attitude there at the end," Theo agreed. "Still, I don't mind having Artie and Holly over."

"They're good kids. Abe, too.." Avery nodded. "The Cardoso boys can help you with a garden, too, if you were serious. They're dryads. Stacy's human, though."

"So you've said."

"Sorry." Avery patted his shoulder. "It was late and we covered a lot."

"I only found out about magic and the rest last night. I'm just still trying to get my brain around it." Theo sank into one of the chairs set on the wide porch and slumped into the cushions.

"Wait, and you said Ivette is, also?" He glanced over at his neighbor's house.

"Yep." Avery nodded. "Though the other side of her family were witches, so she has different gifts." He perched on the top step and leaned his back against the railing so he could face Theo. "There are a lot of us in this neighborhood. In the whole town, really, but especially here. Not just fae, either, obviously."

Theo felt like he had fallen down the rabbit hole, but he asked anyway. "Like dryads?"

Avery nodded, then grinned puckishly. Which Theo realized was an even more fitting description than he first thought, dammit.

"And shifters, like Mateo." Avery said. "The Three-Legged Wolf is named after the guy who opened it. Lost a limb in World War Two."

"He lost... Am I sitting down?" Theo closed his eyes and focused on his breathing. He remembered vaguely an article he wrote about a scientific study on meditation, and one of the people he interviewed showed him the technique. He'd use any damn trick he could think of right now. "Literally everything I know about the world has been kicked around like sand toys at the beach."

A warm hand landed on his knee and he opened his

eyes to find Avery crouched next to him, peering up into his face with concern. "It's a lot. But I'm not going to lie to you or hide things from you now. Most of the people that live in the older houses, that lived here before that developer jerk showed up aren't human. Or at least aren't fully human. Some of the ones in the new places aren't human, but it's harder for us to live under Marielle's thumb. Her rules seem almost deliberately made to drive us away. Almost."

"And Marielle? Is she part demon?" Theo cocked an eyebrow.

Avery barked out a laugh. "Oh man, no. Totally human, but I would definitely believe it."

"Demons exist?" Theo was actually worried now.

"Not that I know of, but I'm just a warrior. That's more Darren's line of questions." Avery grinned. "Part demon, man. I'm totally using that."

"I won't even charge you for it."

Avery plopped down on the porch's floor and leaned his shoulder against the leg of the chair. "You going to be okay, though? I know it's a lot, and not everyone who finds out is very comfortable with the new knowledge."

Theo blinked down at him. "You know there's another chair, right?"

Avery shrugged and took a sip of his coffee.

Theo stared out at the lush, emerald lawn. He let himself imagine a bit of a garden along the fence. Maybe some azaleas and roses. He remembered what Ivette had said and decided to ask her again what plants she suggested. It seemed likely that there was more than just being pretty for her to recommend them.

A car drove by, and another neighbor walked past pushing a stroller with a sleeping toddler in it. They smiled and waved, and Theo and Avery both waved back. Just over a month ago he had been living out of boxes in his parents' house. Four weeks ago, Theo had moved here and felt alone in this large, untidy house crammed full of things he didn't want or need and felt like the disorganized mess of cluttered garbage matched his life. Now?

He closed his eyes again and felt the energy of a house with people in it. Magical bits and bobs were squirreled away all over the house, waiting for him to discover them. Books full of strange and wonderful information sat on shelves next to Garfield's notes that Theo was thinking of organizing. Disorganized and cluttered, yes, but it wasn't garbage to him anymore.

Small sounds reached him from inside and he wondered if Darren and Quinn were in the kitchen sorting out dinner or if they were still buried in that history book. He could sense Avery sitting next to him, just a few inches away and almost hovering in his concern that Theo was about to freak out. Avery was worried about a friend, and not because he could get something out of it, and wasn't that a hell of a thing?

Theo opened his eyes again.

"I would rather know the truth of the world than live blindly stumbling around in it, if that makes sense. But yeah. It's a lot. My whole life has changed pretty dramatically in the last few weeks, though, so why not just keep rolling with it?"

Avery's smile brightened his whole face. Hell, it brightened the whole porch. Combined with that Caribbean blue hair it felt like a tropical sunrise.

"Really?"

Theo nodded.

There was a small crash from inside, and Avery jumped up. "Oh, shit. I hope Darren's not trying to cook.

He'll burn the whole place down!" He went running inside to prevent some unknown disaster.

Theo stood to slowly follow, with a silent thank you to his crazy old great-uncle. This wasn't such a bad place to be, after all.

ACKNOWLEDGMENTS

This story has been a long time coming. I started thinking over the idea that inspired this book before I even started the FPAA series.

It all started with a backstage conversation while a few of us waited for a show to start. My fellow spot-op had fallen down a rabbit hole of research on people who build and maintain haunted houses. I don't remember any of the details of the conversation at this point, but I all of us wondering what these folks' homes looked like, and if their HOA board took exception to the shrieks and wails of electronic ghosts and virtual witches.

I also remember all of us effectively dissolving into giggles as we got sillier and sillier about things the HOA would object to: witch cauldrons decorated for Christmas. Noise violations for poltergeists. No werewolves allowed over 25 pounds.

I am not anywhere near as funny as my old coworkers, and sadly, I could never quite get a comic story out of the whole idea. But eventually Theo started talking to me, then Avery chimed in and the rest, as they say is history.

I would like to thank Curtis and Jared for the initial inspiration, and for being awesome co-workers. Thanks to my brother Gage for not only naming the Three-Legged Wolf, but for designing its logo AND the logo for the Last Pot Cafe! To Stuart, as always, thanks for your patience and for the alpha-read. Sara Tunder, your critique alternately made me curse when you pointed out something wrong, and cackle with satisfaction when you reacted exactly like I hoped a reader would. Thank you so much. And of course, thanks to my new editor Robin J Samuels at Shadowcat Editing. Sorry about the wierd spellings.

If you enjoyed hanging out in Whitelake as much as I did, please take a moment to leave a review! Every review or star rating makes an enormous difference, especially to an indie author. And fear not, there are more adventures coming.

ABOUT THE AUTHOR

Katherine Kim is a lifelong lover of fantasy. She started early, being read Tolkien as bedtime stories, which honestly explains a lot. More recently she's been drawn to more urban fantasy stories through both books and television, and reading continues to be a passion. She is an American that lives and writes in Tokyo, with her family.

If you liked this book, I hope that you'll leave me a review! I read every review and it makes a huge difference to me and to my work, but even just a few stars would make my day. You can also join my newsletter for news, announcements, and snippets of my life in Tokyo, or my Patreon for sneak peeks at my works in progress and a new short story every month!

BOOKS BY KATHERINE KIM

The Demon Guardian

A Demon's Duty

A Demon's Sanction

A Demon Saved

The Riverton Demons

Personal Demons

Spirits of Los Gatos

Sarah's Inheritance

A Spirit's Kindred

Finding Insight

Brewing Trouble

Spiritkind

Federal Paranormal Activities Agency

Quick Study (Prequel)

Caroline's Internship

In The Blood

Heavy Traffic

Vampire's Curse

Fighting Fire

Lightning Source UK Ltd.
Milton Keynes UK
UKHW010752060223
416537UK00008B/2040

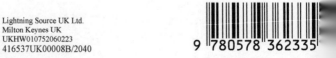